SHOWDOWN

"Which's it to be, Smith?" the dandy named Hayward demanded. "I'll give you a count of five. One—!"

Instead of taking the count further, Hayward grabbed for his gun.

An interested spectator, Dad Derham, saw the treacherous move and wondered how Smith could hope to counter it without a trigger finger on either hand.

Having watched Hayward's eyes, Smith knew what the other was planning. His trained reflexes took over. . . . With the dandy's revolver still lifting from leather, Smith relaxed the grip of his thumb. The hammer sprang forward. Flame rushed from the Colt, and the discharged load ripped into the gambler's forehead. With the back of his skull shattered open, he slammed into the counter.

Also by J. T. Edson:

THE NIGHTHAWK
NO FINGER ON THE TRIGGER
THE BAD BUNCH

SLIP GUN

J. T. Edson

A DELL BOOK

For Terry Barratt, who drives his bus
like the Kid rides Midnight

Published by
Dell Publishing
a division of
Bantam Doubleday Dell Publishing Group, Inc.
666 Fifth Avenue
New York, New York 10103

ISBN: 0-440-20772-X

Reprinted by arrangement with the author

Printed in the United States of America

Published simultaneously in Canada

November 1990

10 9 8 7 6 5 4 3 2 1

OPM

1

The Man Who Hated Rain

Going by the mass of dark clouds that spread across the sky from over the Antelope Hills, there might be a storm during the night. Even if the storm did not break, rain was sure to fall.

Waxahachie Smith hated rainy weather.

No matter how carefully Smith wrapped himself in his yellow oilskin "slicker," the water always found a way through to run down his neck. Worse than that, rain invariably made his trigger fingers ache like hell. Which was mighty strange. His trigger fingers must have long since rotted into nothing at the place where he had left them on the banks of the Rio Grande.

Give that crazy son of a bitch Doc Grantz his full and rightful due, though. He had taken off the fingers as neat as a man could ask for, leaving sufficient skin to fold as pads over the places where they had been. Once the original pain of the removal had ceased, the stumps only troubled Smith when it rained. No fancy Eastern sawbones, working in a real hospital with all the latest surgical aids, could have done a better job.

It had almost been a pity to kill Doc Grantz.

In fact, some folks came right out and claimed that Smith had acted a mite ungrateful by killing him. Any qualified doctor ought to be within his rights to amputate injured fingers, toes, arms or legs, if doing so would save his patient's life. While agreeing in principle, Smith had still put sawdust in the doctor's beard and made wolf bait of him.

At the time that the amputations had been carried out, Smith's forefingers were in no way endangering *his* health or life. It was just that they could squeeze a Colt's trigger too well for the Fuentes brothers' peace of mind. So perhaps in one way the removal of his fingers could be called necessary. By causing it to be done, the brothers had hoped to save *their* lives. When all they had wanted was to take over the Texas border town of Flamingo, Smith and his Colt stood between them and the citizens. Everybody had known that sooner or later a showdown must come. Most had guessed which way it would go—against the Fuentes boys.

Rich and unscrupulous, the brothers might have had Smith bushwhacked; but killing a Texas Ranger—which he had been at the time—ranked as real bad medicine. So they had arranged for his food to be drugged one night. When he had regained consciousness, no forefingers remained to press a trigger. Yet when it rained, even though four years had passed since the operation, the missing digits still throbbed painfully.

So Smith hated rain, for it brought back memories he would rather forget.

Moving at an easy pace between Smith's long legs as he posted to its trot,* the line-backed *bayo-lobo* gelding suddenly snorted and tossed its head. The man made no attempt to reach for a weapon, knowing that his mount's actions did not warn of impending danger. Rather it had smelled its own kind ahead, their scent being carried over the next ridge by the same wind which spread the clouds.

Damn those clouds, with their threat of rain to bring torment to his nonexistent fingers. Smith much preferred to work in the heat, dust and sweat of New Mexico or Arizona, where the average rainfall was low. If the request from Wyoming had been less urgent, or the advance payment smaller, he might have ignored it. Trouble was, like a fool he had accepted the money. His reputation would suffer if he failed to show up at Widow's Creek and find out what the prospective employer had to offer.

Topping the ridge, Smith found that he had read the gelding's signal correctly and there was no cause for alarm. Going by the cluster of whipsaw-plank buildings and the type of horses roaming aimlessly in the two large pole corrals, he had arrived at Gilpin's

---

* For a description of posting at a trot, read *Under the Stars and Bars.*

stagecoach way station. Not a surprising discovery, nor a remarkable piece of cross-country navigation, seeing that he had been following the stagecoach trail from the time he had left the railroad at Laramie. Even before he nudged the gelding with his heels, he felt its pace quicken. Most likely it had scented grain and fresh hay, so knew that the end of its day's work was in sight. So he guided it down the slope in the direction of the largest of the buildings.

Attending to his chores in the big combined stable and barn, old Dad Derham listened to the approaching horse with an attitude of anticipation. Always a student of his fellow men, he found that the somewhat menial post as hostler on a way station presented many opportunities to carry out his studies. Trouble being that each passing year saw a growing difficulty in forming accurate conclusions.

Time was a feller could tell, near enough, where a stranger hailed from and how he earned his living by his clothing and horse rigging. There had been few enough types of work then and most of them required specialized forms of dress. With the development and expansion of the cattle industry, cowhands tended to mingle styles in a mighty confusing manner. Then there were all the nesters, farmers and other settling folks coming from back East. The Good Lord alone knew how you pegged them down to their home range by what they wore.

The hooves stopped and leather creaked as weight was transferred from it to the ground. Stepping out of the empty stall he had just finished cleaning, Derham watched Smith lead the gelding through the big double doors. A grunt of satisfaction left the old-timer. No mistaking this traveler's place of origin. Most conservative and state-proud of all cowhands, a Texan invariably clung to the traditional fashions of his home range.

Not, Derham admitted, that the stranger was a cowhand. Which raised the question of what he might be.

Six foot two in height, lean and whang-leather tough-looking as a steer fed on greasewood, the stranger wore a low-crowned, wide-brimmed, black J.B. Stetson hat as Texas as the Lone Star flag and "Remember the Alamo!" Framed with neatly trimmed reddish-brown sideburns, the face sheltered by the hat was too rugged to be termed handsome. Tanned by long exposure to the sun, it had hard, grim lines and cold, watchful brown eyes. That was the face of a man who had suffered.

Under his buttoned-up wolfskin jacket, he wore a neatly knotted black string tie and gray flannel shirt. Coming from beneath the jacket, which concealed whatever kind of gun belt he might be wearing, blue-jean legs ended tucked into flat-heeled brown Wellington half boots.* Brown leather gloves covered his hands. Not the heavy gauntlets a man from the thorn bush or cold-weather countries might wear, but lighter and more flexible. Gamblers often sported such gloves, to keep their hands soft for manipulating a deck of cards. The man was not a professional gambler. That tanned face had not been gained sitting all night at a card table and sleeping most of the day.

Maybe his mount would supply a clue.

By its conformation and size, the gelding would be better suited to long traveling than for the fast-twirling, rapid footwork needed when working cattle. The wide two-ear bridle sported fancy-stitched leatherwork and the shanks of the curb bit took the form of plump, shapely feminine buttocks and legs. Although functional in design, the low horned, double-girthed saddle had decorative carving on its fork, cantle, skirt, upper-flank skirt and fenders; *rosaderos,* † the man would call the latter. The horn's embossed top and the conchas which held the saddle strings had the dull, solid glint of silver. On the left side of the saddle, pointing to the rear, the butt of a rifle showed from its boot. A bulky bedroll and yellow slicker hung behind the cantle, but no coiled rope dangled from the fork. That kind of rig had been born in Texas, where a feller tied fast his rope and figured to hand onto anything he caught in its loop.

For all that, taken with the low-heeled footwear, the absence of a coiled rope on the saddle revealed that the stranger did not earn his living handling cattle.

* Not the modern, waterproofed rubber variety, but the style made popular by the Duke of Wellington.

† Rosaderos: vertical, wide leather shields stitched behind the stirrup leathers.

Unfortunately, it did not help Derham place the stranger. Not entirely, anyway. By removing one possibility, it opened up another. The man walked with an economy of motion, silent and somehow seeming as graceful as a cat. There was an alert air about him, such as a man with many enemies always showed. Derham had never seen a gunfighter who did not. Seeing how he carried his gun might have furnished information, but the jacket prevented that. If he had enemies, he clearly did not expect to come across them around the way station. The buttons would have been unfastened, allowing uninterrupted access to his revolver, if he did.

By the time Derham had drawn that conclusion, the newcomer had almost reached him. Satisfying his curiosity about the other could only be done indirectly. So the old hostler elected to try a conventional opening to a conversation which might prove instructive.

"Looks like—" Derham began amiably.

"Yeah," Smith interrupted. The last thing he wanted was to be reminded about the state of the weather. "Can I put up my horse in here?"

"Use that empty stall," Derham answered stiffly. Age ought to carry certain privileges and command some respect. His tone showed that he resented the curt response. "Put him in, if it suits you."

Just how it happened, Derham could not say, but his last words had been addressed to the stranger's back. Footsteps thudded outside, coming toward the barn. In a swift, silent movement, Smith had dropped the gelding's reins and moved to face the open double doors. He stood so that he could look across the back of his horse at whoever entered. While looking, he began to peel off his gloves.

Being wise in such matters, Derham realized that the stranger's actions had not been made as a further snub to him. They were merely the kind of precautions, like removing the gloves, that a gunfighter would take.

The young men strolled into the barn as if they owned it. Tall, bulky, they wore a hybrid mixture of town and range clothes, with Colts in low-hanging, tied-down holsters. Going by their swaggering attitudes, they considered themselves to be important citizens.

"Hey, you. Hostler there," called the taller of the pair. "Try 'hostling' some and get our hosses ready."

"Right sharp too," the second new arrival went on, darting a challenging look Smith's way. "We ain't got all day."

"I'm tending to this gent," Derham objected.

"He don't mind waiting," declared the first speaker.

Smith's cold, unfriendly eyes studied the pair and he assessed their quality like a rancher picking culls out of a herd. He did not need much deep thought to classify them. No matter where one rode west of the Mississippi River, their kind could be found. Small-town loafers, would-be hardcases, reared on tales of the old-time gunfighters and desperate to prove themselves in that same magic-handed category. Given the right conditions, they could be as dangerous as a stick-teased diamondback rattlesnake. Let them take an inch of liberty with you and they would grab for a mile. Wanting no trouble with them, Smith acted accordingly.

"I *do* mind waiting," he stated, dropping the gloves into his jacket's side pockets and stepping clear of the horse.

"Yeah?" grunted the taller hardcase. "Well, he'll get 'round to you when he's through with us."

" 'Cepting I don't figure on waiting that long," Smith replied. "I'll be needing grain, water and hay, mister."

Watching the byplay, Derham felt uneasy and a mite disappointed. He had decided that the newcomer was a gunfighter and felt that the other was trying to spoil his summation. Instead of unbuttoning his jacket, the man had thrust his hands deep into its pockets. Glancing down, the old-timer failed to detect any bulge that would hint that either pocket held a weapon. A man ought not to go up against Billy and Angus McCobb unless he was full ready to protect himself.

Taking in Smith's posture, Billy McCobb flashed a knowing wink at his smaller, younger brother. Like Derham, Billy had looked carefully for signs of the stranger holding a gun concealed in one pocket. Billy felt sure he was not. Maybe that feller figured to look hard and ornery, but he missed impressing Billy by a good country mile. He needed teaching a lesson in Sweetwater County manners, which the brothers would be right pleasured to give him.

"I'm saying the hostler sees to us first," Billy announced, advancing slightly ahead and to the right of Angus. "So you can just set back and wait on your betters, feller."

"Counting there was any such," Smith drawled, keeping his hands in his pockets. "I don't see any of 'em around."

"Maybe you need something to open your eyes!" Billy barked. "Like a crack 'tween 'em with a Colt's barrel."

"You'd have to take it out afore you could do that," Smith pointed out.

"Which's easy enough done!" Billy snapped, right hand dropping toward the holstered revolver as he strode into range for carrying out the threat.

Smith moved while Billy was declaring his intentions. Unlike the young hardcase, who had telegraphed every move, the Texan gave no hint of what he meant to do. Leaving his hands where they were, Smith bent his right knee slightly. Up swung his left leg until its knee almost touched his chest and the foot was vertical to the ground. All in the same flashing motion, the sole of Smith's boot caught Billy on the chest and shoved hard. Taken by surprise, Billy staggered by his brother and landed on his rump with a solid thud.

From delivering the attack, Smith dropped the boot to the floor and used it as a pivot. Seeing the Texan apparently turning away, Angus lunged at him. If the younger brother believed that he was coming unexpectedly, he received rapid disillusionment. Balancing on his left leg, Smith swung his right around and stabbed it rearward. It rammed with speed, accuracy and considerable force against Angus' solar plexus. Letting out a croaking yelp of pain, Angus changed his advance into a retreat. Stumbling backward, he tripped over Billy's feet and fell on top of his brother. They subsided in a heap, to Derham's undisguised delight.

Foul language billowed up from the McCobb boys as they rolled apart. Still seated on the hard-packed dirt floor, they directed their thoughts to wiping out the insult piled upon their family's honor. With hands grabbing toward holsters, they turned angry eyes in search of their assailant. Doing so proved to be one of the few sensible acts in two otherwise misspent lives.

From heaving Angus after Billy, Smith brought his left leg down

in the first of three strides which carried him to his horse's near
flank. His hands, stripped of their gloves, left the pockets. The
right flashed forward to close around the wrist of the rifle's butt.
At the same moment, the left slapped the gelding on the rump.
Snaking its head aside, to avoid stepping on the trailing reins, the
horse walked into the empty stall. By doing so, it drew the saddlebag away from the rifle. As soon as the barrel cleared leather,
Smith spun on his heel in the brothers' direction. Swinging the rifle
around, he caught its foregrip in his left palm. He halted with his
weapon dangling before him in both fists.

Admiration and satisfaction flickered on Derham's seamed old
features as he watched Smith hand the McCobb boys their sup-
plies. Every move had clearly been planned in advance and carried
out with commendable precision. Putting his hands in his pockets
had been smart, not foolish, lulling the brothers into a sense of
false security. Derham had never seen a feller who could handle his
feet in such a fancy, effective manner.

Glancing at the rifle, the hostler felt puzzled. At first sight it
looked like an old Henry, with the barrel-long tubular magazine
completely exposed. Its excellent condition suggested that it had
been made long after Oliver Winchester stopped production on the
Henry in favor of the more advanced models. Closer observation
showed that it lacked the usual Winchester's lever and had a
foregrip, shortened to a piece of wood just large enough to be
grasped by its user's left hand. Derham might have noticed other
things, but the McCobbs' behavior attracted his attention.

"Get the—" Billy was saying.

"If you try to pull those guns," Smith put in, and the rifle's
muzzle tilted into line between the brothers, ready to turn either
way, "I'll kill you both."

There was no bombast in the words, only a plain statement of
fact. With a cold, chilling sensation, Billy realized that he had gone
in when the water ran high over the willows. A quick glimpse of
his brother's face told him that Angus shared his sentiments. Taking their hands away from the guns, they came slowly to their feet.
Still the rifle remained pointing in their direction. The situation
called for tact, not muscle.

"You'd best tell him who we are, old man," Billy ordered, trying to retain his habitual tough tone.

"They're Sheriff McCobb's nephews, mister," Derham introduced.

"Deputies!" Billy corrected coldly. "Nephews" did not carry a sufficiently impressive connotation at that moment. Turning what he hoped to be an officially threatening eye on Smith, he continued, "And we're on law business, stranger."

"Which nobody's stopping you doing," Smith pointed out. "I'll take the water and grain for starters, friend."

"That's im—imp—im—!" Angus spluttered, trying to remember an imposing legal term he had heard used by his uncle.

"Impeding an officer in the right and lawful execution of his sworn duty's what you mean," Smith supplied. "And, afore you tell me I'm doing that, you pair's near on been guilty of felonious assault on a law-abiding citizen, threatening behavior and malabusement of civic authority as covered in Amendment Eleven, Twenty-Three, Sixty-One of the Constitution."

Although the rifle had turned away from them while Smith was speaking, the brothers refrained from further hostilities. They were impressed by his quick and thorough command of legal phraseology. Whatever that "malabusement of civic authority" might be, it sounded important—and liable to make bad trouble for lawmen caught doing it. The brothers eyed Smith with renewed interest and some concern, wondering who the hell he might be. He knew the law and handled that rifle real good. Maybe he was a peace officer in transit between jobs. Or, worse still, he might be a U.S. marshal touring Wyoming Territory to find out how it stacked up for statehood.

Whoever the stranger might be, he exhibited no concern over what the brothers might do next, nor for their uncle's, the sheriff's, possible wrath. If he should be a U.S. marshal, he packed a whole heap more political say-so than any sheriff, and Uncle Horace would not want him riled. It might be smarter to let the matter drop, cut their losses and depart before worse happened to them.

"Come on, Angus," Billy snapped, sounding briskly and artificially efficient as he made his second wise decision in one day, a record which he would probably never again equal. "Let's get moving, we don't have time to waste here."

"We sure don't," the younger McCobb agreed. "Unc—The sheriff's counting on us to see the stage comes in safe."

Having convinced themselves—if nobody else—that they were withdrawing from the unpleasantness by their own choice, the brothers slouched across to the inverted V-shaped wooden burro erected along the left sidewall. They collected their saddles, went in and entered their horses' stalls.

"You can lend them a hand," the Texan told Derham. "If you're so minded."

"I ain't," answered the old-timer. "Boss'd charge my time to the county if I did. Which, being a taxpaying citizen, I ain't fixing to see my hard-earned money wasted a-pampering the sheriff's shirt-tail kin. What can I get for you?"

"Nothing," grinned Smith and joined the gelding in the stall. "But the horse here can use some grain, hay and water."

Cackling appreciatively, Derham ambled away. Smith slid the rifle back into its saddlebag, removed his jacket and hung it over the dividing wall. At the other end of the line of stalls, the McCobbs kept up a too loud conversation and acted as if they had intended doing their own saddling from the beginning. Clearly they had no intention of making more trouble. The gist of their conversation—designed, Smith guessed, to mollify him—was that any hoot owl stupid enough to try robbing a stagecoach under their protection would rapidly and permanently learn the error of his ways. While Smith harbored considerable doubts on that subject, he kept his comments to himself.

Derham had been sufficiently impressed by Smith to overlook the other's earlier brusque conduct. So he took a bucket and filled it with fresh-pumped water, then mixed a meal in a new feed bag. By the time he returned, carrying the bucket in one hand and bag in the other, the McCobbs were leading their horses from the barn.

Going toward the stall where Smith stood rubbing the gelding's back with a fistful of straw, the hostler satisfied some more of his curiosity and gave himself another puzzle. Removing the jacket had exposed Smith's calfskin vest. It also presented the old-timer with the first view of his gun belt. As when Smith had faced the McCobbs with hands in pockets, Derham felt a sense of anticlimax. The belt was higher on Smith's waist than those favored by real fast men. Carrying a Colt Civilian Model Peacemaker with its staghorn butt reversed, an excellently made, contour-fitting Missouri Skintite-style holster rode at an extreme forward tilt just behind his right hip.

In all Derham's experience, which stretched back over more years than he cared to consider, he had never seen a gun carried in such a manner. Other details about Smith's armament might have struck the hostler, but he became aware of something which drove all thoughts of it from his head.

Dropping the straw, Smith walked by the saddle which hung on the wall near his jacket. Derham was holding out the feed bag and the Texan reached over the gate to take it from him. Idly the hostler glanced down as the transfer was being made. Then his eyes swiveled from Smith's extended right hand to the tanned face and back in what would eventually become known as a double take.

Where the three sections of the first digit should have been, only a small, puckered pad of flesh remained. Derham decided that must be the reason for the stranger's unconventional method of toting the Colt, he drew it cross-hand with his left.

Thinking back to the newcomer's first unsociable response—and forgetting that Smith had been wearing gloves—Derham decided that he had expected some comment about his injury. A man who had suffered such a loss would not want reminding of it. So the hostler relinquished the feed bag and schooled his face into an expression which he hoped would register disinterested, unseeing nonchalance.

All Derham's ability as a poker player was needed a moment later. Taking hold of the feed bag's strap with his left hand, ready to fix it on the gelding's head, the stranger showed that it too had lost its trigger finger. Only by a considerable effort did the old hostler hold down an exclamation of surprise.

"I'll get you some hay," Derham offered, setting down the bucket.

Straightening up, he stared at the Texan. Memory came to the old-timer, of stories which he had previously discounted as newspaper lies, about a man who had lost both trigger fingers and yet still followed the trade of hired gunfighter.

Could the stranger be that man?

Certainly the loss of the two fingers did not greatly handicap him. He had removed his gelding's saddle and bridle quickly enough. Come to that, he had displayed considerable speed in producing the rifle from its bag. No wonder that the McCobb boys had suspected nothing. The way that long Texan handled the rifle, he might have had two extra fingers a hand instead of one less.

Derham suddenly became aware that he was staring at the stranger; showing all too much interest when dealing with a man who might earn his keep by selling his gun savvy.

"Thanks," the Texan said, showing no annoyance at the scrutiny. "And you're figuring right. I'm Waxahachie Smith."

2

The Man from Schuyler, Hartley and Graham

"I'm right sorry for staring thatways, Mr. Smith," Derham apologized. "That must've been a bad accident."

"It was bad, but it wasn't an accident," the Texan replied, and his tone warned that the subject must be forgotten. "Say, were them two ham-headed yacks for-real deputies?"

"There's some argument on that," the hostler admitted. "You sure handed them a surprise. Hey, what's that there mal—whatever you called it?"

"Malabusement of civic authority?" Smith grinned. "I dunno. I made it up, but it sure sounds like it means plenty. Why'd the sheriff have them here, is he expecting trouble?"

"Naw!" Derham sniffed contemptuously. "Allows that with all the folks headed for Widow's Creek, the stages'd be sweet pickings for hoot owls. Now me, I reckon he don't go for keeping 'em 'round Green River for fear the taxpayers start figuring he's feeding his kin outen their pockets."

"Such doings wouldn't be tolerated back in Texas," Smith declared. "So, there's big doings in Widow's Creek then?"

"They're fixing to throw the biggest, fanciest county fair Wyoming Territory's ever seed, all I hear be true. Yes, sir, their mayor's—"

"Gilbert! Gilbert Derham!" screeched a tinny female voice. "If you want anything to eat, quit loafing in the barn and get in here."

"That's me wife," the hostler informed Smith. "She don't understand me. Or she do, which's a danged sight worse. I'll get the hay."

Despite the waiting meal, Derham hovered around until Smith

had finished attending to the gelding's needs. After donning his coat and gloves, Smith left the stall carrying his saddle.

"There'll be somebody around all night?" the Texan inquired as he hung the rig and bridle over the burro.

"Sure," the hostler confirmed. "Couple of the boys sleep in here."

Freeing his bedroll, Smith tucked it under his left arm and drew out the rifle with his right hand.

"Ain't never seed a Winchester like that one," Derham hinted.

"Maybe that's 'cause it's a Colt New Lightning," Smith replied amiably. "What they call Elliott's trombone slide-action. This here's one of the first. I had it fitted out special."

Taking a closer look as Smith held the rifle for his inspection, Derham received yet another surprise. Not only was the traditional Winchester lever missing—hardly surprising, considering the rampant colt motif engraved on the handgrip and words COLT'S LIGHTNING .44.40 CAL inscribed on the barrel near the frame—but the weapon had neither trigger guard nor trigger.

"Gilbert Derham!" yelled the woman, before the hostler could comment on the phenomenon. "You get in here, or I'll throw it to the hawgs."

"Maybe I'd best go," the old-timer remarked. "She's likely to do it and I don't have a thing agin them hawgs."

"I'm through here," Smith replied, watching the horse munching at the hay, the feed bag having been emptied and removed. "Now I can tend to my needs."

Going to the big main building, Smith entered and secured his accommodation. He left his rifle and bedroll on the rope bedstead allocated to him in the men's communal quarters. Returning to the porch, he removed jacket and gloves so that he could wash in the basin which stood on a bench by the front door. While drying himself on a somewhat cleaner than usual roller towel attached to the wall over the basin, he heard the sound of hooves and wheels. Looking around, he saw a big, heavily mustached, florid-faced man driving up in a buggy. From his bowler hat and gray overcoat, open to show a matching suit and gaudy necktie, taken with the trunk strapped to the back of the vehicle, he might be a drummer of some kind. Nodding a greeting to Smith, the man went by and halted outside the barn.

With his hands dry, Smith gathered his property and entered the combined bar and dining room. He selected a small table by one of the windows and sat at it. The owner had warned him that no food would be available until the stage arrived, so he settled in what comfort he could manage to wait for it. Letting the jacket hang on the back of his chair, he slid on his gloves. The first drops of rain splattered against the windowpanes and he felt the expected twinge of pain commence.

Experience had taught Smith that he could forget the pain if he found something to occupy his mind. So he took his wallet from the jacket's inside pocket and extracted a buff-colored telegraph message form. Opening the paper, he laid it and the wallet before him on the table.

"W. SMITH. MARSHAL'S OFFICE. ALBERTSVILLE, NEW MEXICO," Smith read. "NEED YOUR SERVICES URGENTLY BY END OF MONTH. IF CAN COME, BANK YOUR TOWN AUTHORIZED TO ADVANCE TWO HUNDRED DOLLARS AS EVIDENCE OUR GOOD FAITH, ALSO RAILROAD FARE TO LARAMIE. W. S. P. JEFFREYS, MAYOR. WIDOW'S CREEK, WYOMING TERRITORY."

Not much to go on there, but Smith had felt justified in investigating. The money had been handed over by the Albertsville banker without batting an eye. If anything, considering that he was one of the city fathers, the banker had probably been pleased with the sign that Smith was leaving.

They were all the same, Smith mused, eager to hire his gun in times of trouble; but even more eager to see him move on once he had hauled their hot chestnuts out of the fire. That was understandable, for his services came higher than the wages paid to an ordinary town marshal. Of course, Smith took chances and handled chores an ordinary town marshal would never be called upon to face. That was why he was hired.

Folks did not like hired gunfighters, even when they brought one in to help them. Such a man provided an answer to difficult problems, or applied a drastic remedy for certain social ills. With the problems solved, or the ills cured, he became an expensive luxury and an unpleasant reminder of things the sober, upright citizens who hired him would rather forget.

All right. So Smith had known what he was getting into when he had first hired his gun. Doing so had seemed to be the only answer to *his* problems. Until he had lost his trigger fingers, his sole trade had been that of peace officer. The skills he had acquired at it were of small use in any other field.

"Easy there!" Smith warned himself silently but sharply. "You always get to thinking that ways when it's raining and your hands hurt."

Even as he gave himself the advice, Smith became aware of a feeling that somebody was watching him. The front door had opened and the scrutiny came from that direction. Swinging his head, Smith found that the dude from the buggy had just entered. For a moment, the Texan thought that he had forgotten to replace his gloves. His hands always attracted attention, which was why he kept them covered. No, he had the gloves on. By his hands lay his open wallet, its well-filled interior exposed to the newcomer's gaze.

"Howdy," greeted the man, bringing his eyes to Smith's face. "We're in for a real wet one tonight, I'd say."

"Looks that way," Smith admitted, and wondered why the hell folks always had to talk about the weather.

"I'm pleased I got here before the storm broke," the man went on.

Crossing to the bar without as much as another glance at Smith's wallet, the man spoke to the big, bulky stationmaster. He would be arranging for his accommodation, Smith guessed. Sure enough, Gilpin took him into the men's bedroom. Replacing the telegraph message in his wallet, Smith returned them to his jacket's pocket. More rain beat at the windows. Like the nagging throb of toothache, the pain grew in his hands. Coming to his feet, he draped the coat over his shoulders and went to the counter.

"Stage should be along soon," Gilpin commented, slouching back to his position behind the bar. "If it's not, I'll have the missus set out your meal."

"*Gracias,*" Smith replied.

Going by the stationmaster's lack of interest in his gloved hands,

Smith guessed that the old hostler had not mentioned his identity. That was lucky. Some folks shied away from giving information to a known gunfighter. Being something of an unknown quantity, Smith might learn about the prevailing conditions around Widow's Creek. Maybe he would even discover the reason he had been sent for. Way station personnel heard much gossip and Gilpin had the look of a man who liked to talk.

"Have something while you're waiting," the stationmaster suggested, reaching under the bar to bring out a bottle and two glasses. Winking as he drew the cork, he went on, "Missus don't cotton to me drinking alone, so you'll be doing me service taking one."

"I've always been told we was sent here to help others," Smith drawled. "Only nobody ever says what the others were sent for. Anyways, all of us fellers should stand together."

"You headed for Widow's Creek?" Gilpin inquired, after they had exchanged salutations over the drinks.

"If I get there," Smith answered, in a noncommittal manner calculated to extract further information about the town and its affairs.

"All I've heard," Gilpin said, "it'll be something to see, that county fair. 'Less there's trouble."

"Should there be?" Smith asked, sensing that he was close to achieving his desire.

"You mix cowhands and nesters, that's trouble," Gilpin replied. "Which'll be a damned shame. Wil Jeffreys's aiming for a celebration that'll make the big county fair they held at Tombstone a few years back look like a church social in a one-hoss village."*

"That so?"

"Yes, sir. Town's staking a whole bundle of cash money on doing it. I'll bet Wil's raising a muck sweat 'n case something goes wrong. Wil's mayor up there and a mighty smart—"

"That's what I like to see!" boomed a voice, cutting Gilpin off just as Smith stood to hear about his prospective employer. "An open bar, with drinks on it. Mind if I join you, gents?"

* For the story of the Cochise County fair, read *Gun Wizard*.

Striding across to the bar, the dude beamed jovially from Smith to Gilpin and back. With his overcoat off and bowler thrust to the back of his head, the man looked even bigger than while riding the buggy. Although he wore a well-cut Eastern suit, with a gold "Dickens" watch chain glinting across the front of his vest, a Western gun belt was cinched about his middle and a Colt Peacemaker rode in a cross-draw holster at its left side.

"Feel free," Gilpin confirmed, producing another glass and filling it.

"Burbury's the name, gents," the dude continued, exuding the professional bonhomie of a drummer. "I sell general merchandise for Schuyler, Hartley and Graham of New York City. And now one of you gents's going to say, 'Why doesn't one of them come selling while the other two mind the store?'"

"I've often wondered about that," Gilpin grinned. "Why don't they?"

"Because they're rich enough to hire poor bastards like me to come and do it," Burbury replied. "I met you when I came in, Mr. Gilpin."

"This's Mr.—" Gilpin began, giving a hint for an introduction.

"Smith," the Texan supplied and grinned. "Damned if I don't change it to Featherstone, or some such, way folks look when I tell them."

"I'll bet you have trouble taking your wife into a hotel where they don't know you," Burbury chuckled. "Had a friend called 'Brown' once and he had to quit taking his wife on the road with him because of it."

"I'm not married," Smith replied, just a touch bitterly. Then he stiffened slightly. There was no sense in brooding about Sally. Her folks had not considered a man without forefingers capable of supporting her and had taken her away from Texas. "But I still have trouble getting into hotels."

"So do I," Burbury admitted. "Anyways, I was never much on 'mistering.' Some'd say I should be, seeing that my pappy done a meanness and had me christened Cedric. My friends call me 'Ric.'"

"Say 'Wax' if it comes easier than 'Smith,' " the Texan offered. "How about having another drink on me, gents?"

"Let me set them up," Burbury requested.

At that moment a stage coach arrived. That put an end to Smith's hopes of learning about Widow's Creek and its mayor. Raising the bar's entrance flap, Gilpin stepped through and headed toward the door. Coming from the kitchen, Mrs. Gilpin joined her husband on the porch to welcome and check the numbers of the guests. Turning, Smith hooked his elbows on and rested his back against the counter. Then, in a casual-seeming gesture, his left hand moved across to grip the fingers of the right glove. Until he saw who had arrived, he figured it best to be ready for trouble. Apparently attaching no importance to the Texan's movements, Burbury continued to lean by Smith's side.

"Wonder if there's anybody on board worth knowing?" the drummer remarked, finishing his drink and setting down the glass.

"Schuyler, Hartley or Graham might be along," Smith suggested.

"Sure," Burbury replied. "You often see folks you don't want to come off a stage."

Pondering briefly on the drummer's cryptic utterance, Smith listened to the commotion outside. Followed by the passengers carrying their overnight bags, Mrs. Gilpin returned. Although the rain was falling heavily, the people from the stage had avoided it until making the brief journey from the stage to the porch.

Neatly dressed in a stylish, but practical, gray serge traveling costume—which emphasized rather than concealed a magnificent hourglass figure—with a dainty hat perched on her somewhat disheveled blond hair, a tall, eye-catching young woman was in the lead. There was a maturity and confidence to her beautiful features and a glint in her eyes that suggested experience mingled with cynicism. She seemed aware of Mrs. Gilpin's cold, distant manner as the other indicated the door to the women's sleeping quarters.

"Now there's a gal who's used to being looked at by men and frowned on by 'good' women," Burbury commented, studying the blonde with frankly lascivious approval. "I'll bet she's in the theater, or works in a saloon."

"Likely," Smith agreed, having formed a similar opinion from the beautiful woman's poise and sensual, almost feline, hip-swaying prowl of a walk. "Mrs. Gilpin sure doesn't cotton to her."

"Nor the other women on the stage, I'll bet," Burbury grinned. "I wouldn't mind 'dovetailing' with her, though."

"Me neither," Smith admitted. "I wonder who got her?"

"I've never been that lucky," Burbury declared. "Last time I 'dovetailed,' it was with a fat widow woman and I thought I'd have to fight my legs free."

Smith grinned sympathetically, while studying the other travelers. When a stagecoach had to carry a large number of passengers, an extra seat would be fitted inside. Those occupying it had to interlock, "dovetail," their knees between the knees of the person who sat facing them. It was not a situation regarded favorably by "good" women compelled to travel that way.

In the assortment of passengers following the blonde was a cross section of the population west of the Mississippi. Two obviously well-to-do dudes and their wives—the latter clearly sharing Mrs. Gilpin's antipathy toward the blonde—headed the party. Behind them ambled a small, black-hatted and dressed man whose austere cast of features suggested that he might be a preacher. A burly farmer in his best go-to-town clothes and undented stovepipe hat, with the narrow, curly brim favored by the Grange, stalked glumly on the heels of a runty, grizzled old-timer who looked like a desert-rat prospector cleaned up a mite for traveling. Clad in sunbonnet, cheap coat and gingham dress, the farmer's wife scuttled in. She darted glances over her shoulder at a trio of flashily and nattily attired drummers who exchanged remarks as they brought up the rear of the group. Unless some of them had been riding on top, they must have been "dovetailing" during the journey.

Seeing the McCobb brothers hovering on the porch, Smith prepared to draw off his glove. They stood aside, allowing the station-master to enter accompanied by a man who must have been their uncle. Carrying a Stetson hat with its crown raised in a Montana peak, Sheriff McCobb was clearly aware of his exalted post in the county. Tall, thickset and overweight, he wore a town suit and Napoleon-leg boots. The star on his jacket's breast pocket glinted as if polished regularly. Slanting down to his right leg, a gun belt supported a Remington 1875 Army revolver.

As the brothers followed their uncle, they scowled in Smith's direction. Gilpin was called over by one of the dudes and Billy stepped up to the sheriff. Holding his voice down, the deputy spoke quickly and Smith knew that he was the topic being mentioned. Joining his brother and uncle, Angus added his quota to the brief conversation. While the trio talked, McCobb fanned his surly, sweating face with the Stetson and looked Smith over from head to toe.

"That lawman seems tolerable took with you, Wax," Burbury remarked.

"Us Texans get folks that way, sometimes," Smith answered. "Well, they do say attack's the best means of defense." With that, he pushed from the bar and strolled toward the McCobbs. "Evening, sheriff."

"Howdy," the peace officer answered, seeming a mite disconcerted. "My neph—deputies tell me they had trouble with you earlier."

"Just a misunderstanding," Smith corrected, conscious that the drummer had followed him from the bar and stood listening to what was said.

"I don't follow you," McCobb began.

"They should have showed their badges, instead of counting on folks knowing they was peace officers," Smith explained. "Which I don't have to tell a lawman of your standing that, according to Article Eleven, Section Twenty-Three, Line Sixty-One of the Wyoming Territorial Charter, every officer of the law, unless on special assignment authorized by his superior, must wear his badge of office visibly at all times. 'Course, they might be on a special assignment—"

"Er—Humph! Yes," the sheriff barked. "They are."

"If they'd said so, instead of rough-talking, I'd've been more inclined to listen," Smith continued. "I don't need to explain to a man like *you* how I can't let just anybody roust me around, sheriff."

"Well, I—" McCobb commenced, hesitantly.

"The Gover—I'm not showing *my* badge, either," Smith went on. "So they wasn't to know."

Being aware of his nephews' natures, the sheriff did not doubt that they had provoked the trouble. Nor had he believed their version when they had told it to explain why they had been delayed in meeting the stagecoach. Like them, he could not place Smith and felt equally impressed by the Texan's command of legal knowledge. McCobb had never seen a copy of the Wyoming Territorial Charter, but had no intention of admitting his ignorance.

"You're working for—?" the sheriff started to say.

"I'm not showing my badge," Smith interrupted pointedly. "It's nothing in your county, sheriff, but I can't say any more."

"Of course not, nor need to," McCobb boomed. "The boys acted a mite hasty and're sorry they did. I hope there's no hard feelings?"

A man on a special assignment for the Governor must not be antagonized.

"Not on my part," Smith answered in the manner of conferring a favor. "They're young is all. But with an officer of your caliber to guide them, they'll grow to be a credit to law enforcement."

"What was all that about?" Burbury inquired as McCobb strode away in a self-important manner.

"I had doings with those two knobheads," Smith replied, watching the sheriff addressing the brothers with *sotto voce* vehemence. Throwing worried looks his way, they brought their badges from under their jackets and pinned them on the lapels. "Let's eat."

"I'm for that," the drummer admitted. "Only not at the big table. Most of them bunch from the stage'd put me off my food. Hey, though, you must know the Wyoming Territorial Charter real well, way you quoted that Article down to its line."

"Let's put it this way," Smith drawled, leading the way to a side table. "I wouldn't even know if they have a Charter, but I figured the sheriff didn't either."

3

A Friendly Game
of Put-and-Take

Having taken seats facing each other, Smith and Burbury turned their attention to the other guests. Smith noticed a sardonic smile flicker to the drummer's face as the passengers gathered at the long main table in the center of the room. Clearly Burbury shared the Texan's feelings at the manner in which the social distinctions were being maintained.

Drawn like iron filings to a magnet, the drummers and the McCobb brothers gathered around the blonde as she sat at the left-hand end of the table. Pointedly, the dudes' wives left several empty chairs between their party and the blonde's. Looking smugly important, Sheriff McCobb placed himself next to the elder male dude. The soberly dressed little man and the old prospector selected places at the opposite end to the blonde. After studying the others, the farmer directed his wife to occupy one of the small side tables.

"I'll bet those dudes're wishing they didn't have their wives with them," Burbury commented. "They keep eyeing that blond gal real interested."

"So do you," Smith pointed out.

"I'm smart," grinned the drummer. "I don't have no wife to bring along."

Mrs. Gilpin's kitchen staff appeared and she told a girl to serve Smith and Burbury. Coming over, the girl set down her loaded tray. While she was handing the Texan a plate of boiled potatoes and stew, the front door opened to admit a man.

Halting just inside the room, the newcomer shook water from his sodden Stetson and subjected the occupants to a wary scrutiny.

He was tall, gaunt, unshaven and clad in dirty range clothes. Unlike the hat, his other garments had only a slight sprinkling of rain on them although his boots were muddy. As his eyes roamed from face to face, he kept his right hand dangling close to the wooden grips of the Peacemaker in its tied-down holster.

Although Smith gave no sign of noticing, he was aware that the man's gaze halted on him for a couple of seconds. Acting casually, the Texan lowered his hands out of the man's sight under the table. Even as he started to ease off the right glove, the eyes left him. From Smith, the newcomer turned to study Sheriff McCobb. Displaying no concern over the peace officer's presence, the newcomer slouched toward a table on the opposite side to the farmer and sat down facing the main door.

"That's a mean-looking bastard," Burbury remarked and grinned apologetically at the girl. "It's Eye-talian for a nice feller, honey."

"Last feller who said it reckoned it was German for somebody's uncle," she replied, passing the drummer a knife, fork and spoon. "There's apple turnover next."

"Did you know that feller, Wax?" Burbury inquired, after the girl had gone to serve the farmer and his wife.

"Can't come out and say 'yes' to that," Smith answered. "Should I know him?"

"Likely not," the drummer admitted, whipping out a large white handkerchief and tucking it like a napkin into his shirt's detachable celluloid collar. "Hey! This stew looks real good. I've had some mighty bad meals at way stations."

"And me," drawled Smith, then started to eat.

"Do you do much traveling?"

"Some. I work for the Smith Land and Cattle Company down in Texas."

"Can't say I've heard of it."

"We've not been going long," Smith explained.

"Good cattle country, Texas," Burbury remarked. "Bet you'll not be sorry to be getting back."

"Yeah," Smith replied flatly. A roar of laughter rose from the blonde's party and he nodded toward them. "Sounds like they're having fun."

"Sounds like," the drummer agreed, and tucked into his stew with evidence of a good appetite.

Two more men entered while Smith and Burbury were waiting for their apple turnover to arrive. Although they each carried a gun in a fast-draw holster, neither exhibited the caution of the earlier arrival. Both were tall, slim and elegantly dressed. The younger had a handsome if sullen face. Under his open slicker, his clothes might have served for an illustration of the latest cowhand fashion. Swarthily good-looking and maybe ten years his companion's senior, the other looked as if he had just left a card game on a Mississippi riverboat. He sported a white, flat-topped, broad-brimmed planter's hat. Removing his cloak coat showed him to have on a cutaway jacket, white frilly-bosomed shirt, string tie and light gray trousers tucked into muddy Wellington half boots.

"Fancy pair," Burbury remarked as the couple walked by and took a side table. "Wonder if the young 'n' ever worked with cattle?"

"His partner sure never handled anything heavier than a deck of cards, or a gun," Smith guessed. "I didn't hear them ride by."

"Or me. Which they'd have to if they'd come east along the stage trail," the drummer replied. "Let's hope the apple turnover's as good as the stew."

Flickering a glance at his companion, Smith felt puzzled. Burbury sat back on his chair, gazing blandly to where the blonde and her party were making a noisy meal. There was something wrong about the drummer. Just what, Smith could not put his finger on. While he acted in an amiable, friendly manner, he still caused the Texan to have an uneasy sensation that all was not as it should be. Maybe it was his habit of asking questions, or making comments which ran parallel to Smith's own thoughts.

With their meal over, Smith and Burbury crossed to the bar. At the main table, various diners rose and left. Laughing and promising to come back, the blonde walked away from her party. Followed by almost every male eye, she disappeared into the women's room. Having been deprived of their mutual bond, the brothers and the drummers separated.

About to follow the drummers to the bar, the brothers were halted by their uncle. Smith had watched the sheriff excuse himself from the dudes and guessed that he would be the reason for Mc-Cobb's actions. Sure enough, the sheriff started to talk quietly but with some emphasis. Smith could not catch the words, but figured McCobb must be warning them about their conduct. When Billy and Angus left their uncle, they went to the far end of the bar. That put the drummers and some distance between them and the Texan, which suited Smith admirably.

Dad Derham took up position behind the bar, a soiled apron over his working clothes. Greeting Smith, he explained Gilpin's absence. Apparently the party of dudes were important Chicago folks, with letters of introduction from the Governor and other civic dignitaries at the capital. So they had been asked to spend the night at the Gilpins' house, instead of having to share the ordinary passengers' accommodation. Having ingratiated himself with the visitors, McCobb had been included in the offer.

"Likely they only fed in here to see how the poor folks live," grinned the old hostler. "Anyways, I don't reckon we'll see any more of them tonight."

"Which I'll live through," Burbury declared. "Who I do want to see is that blond gal."

"You mean Lily Shivers?" Derham asked. "She's some gal. Runs the Happy Bull saloon in Widow's Creek. Her and Wil Jeffreys don't get on too good."

"How about some service, barkeep?" called one of the drummers.

"Be right there," Derham promised.

"Afore you go," Burbury said. "Do you know that mean-looking cuss there?"

"Nope," the old-timer admitted. "I could guess what he is, though."

"And me," Burbury admitted. "How'd he come in?"

"Dunno," Derham replied, and stumped off to answer a further request for service from the three drummers.

"You seem tolerable interested in that *hombre,*" Smith remarked to Burbury.

"His kind make me uneasy," the burly man confessed. "I'm carrying a fair-sized wad of folding money. Enough to make a holdup worth trying."

Leaving their wet hats and outer jackets at the table they had used, the gambler and his dandy-dressed companion crossed to the bar. They took up positions between Smith and the trio of drummers.

"Howdy, gents," the gambler said, addressing the latter. "Would I offend you if I asked you to take a drink with us?"

"We've never been offended by that," grinned the largest of the three.

"I'll have a bourbon," the dandy ordered when asked to name his poison.

"Not here, you won't," Derham replied. "Boss don't cater for eddicated thirsts, mister."

"Then he won't mind if I drink my own," the dandy stated, pulling a silver flask from the inside pocket of his fancy fringed-buckskin jacket.

"If he does, he'll tell you," Derham answered. "It don't make no never-mind to me what you drink."

With the round of drinks bought, the gambler set a conversation going. Introductions were made loud enough for Smith to learn that the gambler was Nolan Hardy and the dandy went by the name of Roy Hayward. After some preliminary chatter, Hardy suggested that they might find a means of passing a couple of hours.

"I never sit in a game against a feller I know plays better'n me," the largest drummer replied warily.

Lowering the flask from his lips, Hayward fixed the speaker with a cold eye and growled, "What's that supposed to mean?"

"Nothing, Roy, nothing," Hardy put in. "That's good, sound sense. I'm the same way. In fact, I prefer a game that does away with the ugly element of skill and lets luck have a full rein."

"Such as?" challenged the middle-sized drummer.

"This," Hardy replied, and laid a small metal object like an eight-sided .50-caliber bullet set on a stick upon the counter.

"What in hell'd that be?" demanded the biggest drummer.

"Just the latest sensation in San Francisco," Hardy replied. "A put-and-take top, it's called."

"How do you use it?" the smallest drummer inquired, staring wide-eyed at the thickness of the wallet from which the gambler paid for the drinks.

"Simplicity itself," Hardy explained, dropping the wallet on the counter and taking up the top. "You see that each face has a letter and figure or 'All' on it. P-1, T-1, P-3, T-3, P-4, T-4, P-All, T-All." While speaking, he turned the faces to show the markings. "To play, you give it a spin with the stick and do whatever the uppermost face tells you. If it says P-1, you put one dime, or whatever you're playing for, into the pot. Say you get T-3 come up, you take three out. When the T-All shows, you rake in the pot. And that's all there is to it."

"Sounds easy," the biggest drummer admitted.

"Only you don't like it!" Hayward spat out, glaring at the man. "Listen, feller, Nolan saved my life one time and I don't let nobody disrespect him."

"Take it easy, Roy," Hardy said in a placating manner. "These gents mean no disrespect. Come on, you and I'll have a game."

"I'd like to give that top a whirl," stated the medium-sized drummer, eyes flickering to Hardy's wallet.

"And me," declared the smallest, clearly sharing his companions' interest.

"Then borrow it and try it out amongst yourselves, gentleman," Hardy offered. "That way you'll be able to see how the game goes."

"I'll bet they don't," Burbury whispered in Smith's ear. "Look at them. They're eyeing that wallet like a deacon watching a pretty gal sinner undress."

"Why sure," drawled the Texan, settling his jacket more firmly on his shoulders. "Did you ever hear tell of that game?"

"Nope. It looks square enough, though. And even up for all.

Unless there's some way a feller can control how that top falls, skill don't come anywheres in it."

"Come on, let's have a go at it," the biggest drummer said. "All of us."

"A dime a point?" Hardy recommended. "We can always go higher later."

"Aw, make it a dollar," grinned the largest drummer. "Hell! Most we can lose at a go's four."

"I'd prefer a dime," Hardy objected.

"That'll make 'em the more set to go for the dollar," Burbury commented. "They'll be sure that he's no edge on them."

The burly man proved to have a sound judgment of character. Brushing aside the gambler's objections, the trio insisted that the stakes be a dollar a point.

"All right," Hardy sighed resignedly. "A dollar it is."

"How many can play?" Billy McCobb called, having followed the conversation.

"Any number," the gambler replied. "That's where put-and-take licks card games. Do you want to come in?"

"Might's well," Billy agreed, darting a glance at the door of the women's quarters. "There's nothing else to do."

"Would anybody else like to come in before we start?" Hardy inquired, looking around. The prospector shook his head and the little, soberly dressed man showed his refusal. So the gambler swung his gaze to Smith and Burbury. "How about you, gentlemen?"

"Not for me," Smith replied, having no wish to be brought into close contact with the McCobbs, especially in a gambling game which he guessed might prove more expensive than the newly introduced players suspected.

"I don't gamble with three kinds of people," Burbury declared, looking at Hayward. "Men, women or children."

Despite his previous touchy behavior, the dandy let the comment pass unchallenged. Taking another drink from his flask, Hayward leaned at Hardy's side and did not attempt to join the game.

"All right then," Hardy said. "Ante up a dollar, gents, and let's see which way the luck's going."

After each of the players had placed a dollar into the pot, one of the drummers made the first spin. Gripping the stick between his right thumb and forefinger, he twirled it in a clockwise direction. Whirling around on the nose of the "bullet," the top collapsed as its momentum ceased.

"Take three!" whooped the spinner, joyfully drawing three dollars from the small pile in the center of the bar. "Here, Fred."

"Put four," muttered the smallest of the trio, and did so.

On the top reaching Billy McCobb, he threw a "P-All," and learned one of the snags to the game. The "All" meant that he must put in an amount equal to the total already forming the pot. Scowling a little, he shoved eleven dollars across the counter and thrust the top in Hardy's direction.

"Here's a take-all for me," the gambler announced, spinning it awkwardly so that it turned counterclockwise, and made a wry face as it settled showing "P-4."

Another "P-All," thrown by the largest drummer, swelled the pot to fifty-two dollars. With that much money at stake, none of the players as much as looked when the blonde came from the women's quarters. After glancing at the bar, she went to sit at the main table.

"Now's your chance," Smith remarked to Burbury. "I'd guess the lady's not used to being by her lonesome."

"You could be right," the man admitted. "Why not come over and see?"

"Two's company," Smith drawled. "Asking to make it up to three's plumb foolish doings."

"I'd like to see that gambling man spin the top again," Burbury replied.

"You'll be making me think you're skirt-'fraid," Smith grinned. "After all the stories I've heard about you drummers, for shame."

"Damn it, now I'll have to go," Burbury groaned. "I can't let us traveling men's good name down."

With that, the burly man strode across to the long table. Doffing his bowler hat with a flourish, he bowed and addressed the blonde. After looking at Burbury, she swung her eyes in Smith's direction. From the man's gestures, Smith formed the opinion he was asking her to join them at the bar. Again Smith felt puzzled by Burbury. Since first seeing her, the drummer had expressed considerable interest in Lily Shivers. Yet, given an opportunity to be alone with her, he seemed determined to throw his chance away.

Something fell from the bar and bounced off the toe of Smith's right boot. Although he felt only a slight tap, it took his thoughts off Burbury's behavior. Looking down, he saw the put-and-take top lying close to his foot. Obligingly, he bent and picked it up.

"My apologies, sir," Hardy said. "It slipped out of my hand. Perhaps fate guided it to you. Why not try a spin and see?"

Glancing at the pile of money on the counter, Smith found that it had increased considerably since Burbury's actions diverted his attention. Somebody obviously had hit a "P-All" and there must have been well over a hundred dollars in the pot. A tempting sum. More so since Smith had not risked anything to take a chance at it. Not that he intended doing so.

"It's not my game," the Texan said, and held out the top to Hardy.

"What's up, meathead?" Hayward demanded. "Ain't Northerners' company good enough for you?"

From all appearances, the bourbon imbibed by the dandy was making itself felt. As he spoke, he thrust himself clear of the bar. Halting with the exaggerated attention to balance often displayed by one feeling the effects of liquor, he scowled menacingly at Smith. Hoping to avoid trouble, Smith placed the top on the counter. Without speaking, he turned his back on Hayward. Before the Texan had taken four strides in Burbury's direction, the dandy's voice came again.

"Don't go turning your back on me like I'm dirt, you three-fingered son of a bitch!"

Slowly Smith started to swing around. While doing so, he removed his right-hand glove and held it in his left fist. Crouching slightly, Hayward stood with his right hand spread talonlike above its revolver's butt. At that moment Smith realized what the dandy had called him. Obviously Hayward was aware of his identity. What was more, knowing it, the dandy seemed set on forcing a showdown.

"That's a hard name, *hombre,*" Smith warned, his voice quietly chilling. "So what've you got in mind now you've said it?"

"I don't take kind to unsociable bastards," Hayward replied. "So you're either going to join the game, or get carried out of here feetfirst."

Immediately the put-and-take players, with the exception of Hardy, began to edge away. Behind the bar, Derham started to move out of the line of fire. The gambler did no more than turn to face Smith, standing so that his right arm and hand were hidden from the Texan by Hayward. It was at Hardy that Smith directed his next words.

"You'd best cool him off, mister. I don't take kind to the names he laid on me; but I'm not looking for fuss and I'll pass them up—this once."

"All we want's a friendly game of put-and-take," Hardy answered. "Trouble being, Roy's a determined young man. You've riled him up and nothing short of you joining in'll satisfy him."

"And if I don't?" Smith inquired.

"I'll damned soon make you!" Hayward promised.

Studying the dandy, Smith knew that he was facing a similar situation to the incident in the barn. If he backed down, Hayward was drunk enough to regard it as a sign of weakness.

Or was he so drunk?

The whole deal felt wrong to Smith. Sharpened by long experience, his instincts sensed a trap. That Hayward knew him had been made clear. He had worn his gloves all the time the dandy was in the room. So Hayward could not have seen his hands that evening. Maybe the dandy hoped to gain a reputation by facing and killing Waxahachie Smith. Only that did not account for those other aspects of the affair which smelled wrong.

One thing was certain. Backing down offered no solution. Apart from other considerations, to do so might encourage the McCobb brothers to resume their abuses. Right then, however, Hayward posed a greater threat than they had. Not only was he standing too far away from Smith to make use of the *savate* techniques which had quelled the McCobbs, but the dandy knew who he challenged. Hayward would not be goaded into coming closer.

"Talk him out of it, mister," Smith told the gambler.

"I can't," Hardy confessed in a tone which meant "I won't."

"Then I will," Smith declared, shrugging the jacket from his shoulders. "How do you stand on that, gambling man?"

"It's between Roy and you," Hardy replied.

"Which's it to be, Smith?" the dandy demanded, and the Texan saw annoyance flicker on Hardy's face at the mention of his name. "I'll give you a count of five. One—!"

Instead of taking the count further, Hayward grabbed for his gun.

An interested spectator, Dad Derham saw the treacherous move commence and wondered how Smith could hope to counter it without a trigger finger on either hand.

4

The Sheriff Investigates

Having watched Hayward's eyes, Smith knew what the other was planning. Another fact had struck the Texan. Those were not the eyes of a man with a gut full of liquor to make him ornery. Hayward was cold sober, no matter how he had been acting.

Even as Smith's mind assimilated the fact, his trained reflexes took over. Turning his right elbow outward and almost to the level of his shoulder, he twisted his hand toward the Colt with the speed of a striking snake. Strengthened by hard exercises, his second and third fingers wrapped firmly about the butt and the fourth digit hooked under its bottom. At the same moment, the web of his thumb wrapped over the hammer's spur. Snapping his elbow in, Smith not only twisted the revolver from its holster but its weight cocked the hammer without further effort by the thumb.

With the dandy's revolver still lifting from leather, the barrel of Smith's Colt turned in his direction. Aiming by instinctive alignment, Smith relaxed the grip of his thumb. Freed from restraint, the hammer sprang forward to plunge its striker into the primer of the waiting cartridge. Flame rushed from the muzzle of the Colt and the crash of detonating powder shattered the silence. Hayward reeled back and to the left, his hand falling away from the gun.

Despite his promise of staying out of the affair, Hardy started to draw his revolver as soon as Hayward's hand moved. Faster than his companion, the gambler cleared his holster an instant after Smith's shot rang out. Already stepping to the left, Hardy found the stricken man blundering between him and the Texan. Snarling a curse, the gambler reversed his direction. Ignoring Hayward's crumpling body, he fixed his attention on Smith—and found that his movements had been anticipated.

Using the Colt's recoil and perfectly adapted balance, Smith thumb-cocked the hammer. As if drawn by magnetic force, the four-and-three-quarter-inch barrel followed the gambler's figure. While Hardy was still attempting to line his own weapon, Smith turned loose a second shot. Angled upward, the discharged load ripped into the gambler's forehead. With the back of his skull shattered open, he slammed into the counter. Killed instantly, Hardy released the revolver and tumbled face forward across Hayward.

Smith followed Hardy down with his eyes. For some reason, his attention was attracted by the mud on the pair's boots. Seeing it reminded him of the man who had arrived shortly before them. The recollection came slightly too late. Even as Smith swung his head around, he found that the gaunt hardcase had stood up and was lining a revolver at him.

"Moxley!" Burbury roared, right hand flashing across to draw his gun.

Hearing the bull-throated bellow, the gaunt man swiveled his head around. What he saw caused him to move his revolver out of alignment on Smith. A shot thundered from by the big table and the hardcase rocked under the impact of lead. About to try to save his life, Smith could not help glancing at the source of his salvation. Smoke rose from the barrel of Burbury's Colt as it reached the height of its recoil kick. Although hit in the body, the gaunt man braced himself against the wall still holding his gun.

For all his city clothing, Burbury handled the Artillery Model Peacemaker with casually competent ease. What was more, he responded to the situation like an experienced gunfighter. Drawing back the hammer, he aimed and squeezed the trigger a second time, driving a bullet into the man's head. Showing the same smooth, trained speed, Burbury again cocked the Colt. He did not relax until his victim let the gun fall and slid limply to the floor.

A deep silence that could almost be felt dropped over the room. It lasted for almost thirty seconds, while the powder smoke swirled away into nothing. Looking around, Smith saw that the farmer's wife had buried her face in her hands. Lily Shivers was on her feet, but exhibited no signs of distress. Neither Derham nor the prospector showed any great emotion. Nor, for that matter, did the soberly dressed little man. The drummers and the McCobbs formed a solid wedge of humanity, having crowded together when they had backed out of the immediate danger area.

"Somebody'd best go tell the sheriff," Burbury suggested, holstering his revolver.

Doing so proved to be unnecessary. Footsteps sounded outside, approaching on the run. Satisfied that he would have no further need for it, Smith returned his Peacemaker to its holster. Then he thrust the glove into his left hip pocket, picked up and was knocking the sawdust from his jacket when the door burst open. Gilpin came through, followed by the sheriff. Significantly, Smith noticed, the stationmaster held a gun while McCobb arrived with empty hands.

"What's been happening?" Gilpin asked, after staring around for nearly half a minute.

At least six voices started to give as many different versions in answer to the stationmaster's question. Neither Smith nor Burbury offered to comment, but the burly man joined the Texan.

"Don't all talk!" Gilpin bellowed, restoring order. He thrust the revolver into his waistband and continued, "All right, Dad, you tell it."

"Ain't that much to tell," Derham replied. "Them two in front of the bar tried to gun Mr. Smith down, helped by the jasper over there on the floor. Only things went wrong for 'em, like you see."

"Who started it?" McCobb put in, suddenly realizing that, as sheriff, he should be conducting the inquiry. "Did you see it, Billy?"

"He didn't do anything to *stop* it," Burbury put in.

Darting a scowl at the burly man, Billy turned his gaze to Smith. The deputy hesitated. Much as he wanted to try to blame the Texan for the shooting, Billy also remembered his uncle's instructions. It might go hard for him if he lied, or made unnecessary trouble for a person of that big jasper's importance.

"We was having a game of put-and-take," Billy explained. "That damn . . . gent didn't want to play, but the cowhand had liquor in him and got mean about it."

"Hey!" yelped Angus, pointing at Smith. "Look at his gun hand. He don't—"

"Was I you," Derham interrupted, "I'd stop talking right there. Boss, this-here's Waxahachie Smith."

Every eye in the room had turned to stare at Smith's right hand. Talk welled up as the old-timer made his announcement. Glaring up at the Texan's face, McCobb opened his mouth. A flush of red rose to the sheriff's cheeks and several seconds went by before he could speak.

"You said you was on a special assignment for the Governor!" McCobb accused indignantly when he regained control of his vocal cords.

"If you think back real careful," Smith drawled, "I didn't say no such thing."

"You're not a—a—!" the sheriff spluttered. "Damn it! You're just a—a—"

"A what, sheriff?" prompted Burbury.

"Damn and blast it!" McCobb blustered, ignoring the question. "I want to know what happened, all of it."

"First off," Burbury answered, before anybody else could speak, "Those three come here figuring to kill Wax Smith."

"Why?" McCobb demanded.

"Now that's a right good question," Burbury praised with blatant mockery and looked at the Texan. "How's about a right good answer, Wax?"

"If you think of one, let me know it," Smith replied. "I never saw any one of 'em afore they walked in here tonight."

"You mean they were perfect strangers?" yelped McCobb.

"Don't know about the others," Burbury put in dryly. "But Arney Moxley was a long ways from perfect. You'll find a wanted dodger on him out of Butte, Montana. Eight hundred dollars, walking or flat on a board."

"You know him?" asked the sheriff.

"I've got a good memory for faces," Burbury answered. "Feller in my line of work needs one."

"Hey, sheriff!" Gilpin put in. "Let me have the bodies moved down to the barn, then get the blood washed away."

"Go to it, Bert," McCobb assented. "Maybe I should search them first?"

"Some'd say that's a smart notion," Burbury said. "Only I'm betting you'll not learn much."

"Why?" the sheriff wanted to know.

"Those boys're top-grade stock, way they handled things. They'll not be carrying anything to say who hired 'em to kill Wax."

"It's my civic duty to look, anyways. Billy, Angus, come lend a hand."

At their uncle's words, the brothers exchanged startled, nervous glances. Up to that moment, they had only been employed in unimportant duties like riding escort for stagecoaches. Traveling self-importantly around the county was poor training for the un-pleasant task ahead. More so when the sheriff gave no sign that he would take other than a verbal part in the search.

"Perhaps I could be of assistance, sheriff?" suggested the small, soberly dressed man. "I am by profession an undertaker."

"Go ahead," McCobb authorized, showing relief. "If you need help, my deputies will give it."

"Thank you," the undertaker said. "Perhaps you could lift the gambling man off the other, gentlemen."

Making a wry face, Billy bent and took hold of Hardy's left sleeve. As the deputy tugged, the gambler's left hand opened and a small metal object fell from it.

"What's that thing?" the sheriff demanded.

"The put-and-take top we was using," Billy replied.

"That one's still on the bar," Burbury pointed out. "He must've had another palmed, Wax."

"Looks that way," Smith agreed.

Obviously the sheriff attached no importance to the extra top, or its mate. Instead he picked up the dead gambler's wallet, which had been laying on the counter during the game, and examined its contents. Without taking an active part in the search, he supervised it to the extent of checking each item produced from the bodies' pockets.

Burbury picked up the top which had fallen from Hardy's hand. Watched by Smith, he spun it a half-dozen times using the awkward-looking counterclockwise twirl of the gambler. The results varied, wins and losses coming up. Setting the top aside Burbury took the other one and repeated the tests employing a clockwise spin.

"Put-three," Burbury said quietly and continued to call the other results. "Put-All, Put-Four, Put-Three, Put-All, Put-Four."

"They're all 'put' and no 'take,' " Smith said quietly. "Try spinning it the other way, Ric."

"Well, that's all," the sheriff announced before the experiment could be carried out. "Two hundred dollars each, wallet on the bar packed out with paper. Gambler had a deck of cards and the other a hip flask."

"He'd been drinking from it, Uncle—" Billy began. He paused, knowing that the sheriff disliked references to the deputies being kinfolk. "That's what made him mean."

"He got ornery if he thought anybody was disrespecting the gambling man," Angus went on. "And with the liquor in him—"

"He wasn't drunk," Smith put in.

"We saw him—"

"Making like he was drinking," Burbury finished for Billy. "You see what's in that flask, sheriff."

"All in good time," McCobb answered. "First, I'd like to hear exactly what came off here."

"You wish me to search the other man, sheriff?" asked the undertaker.

"Huh?" McCobb grunted. "Oh, sure. Go help the gent, Billy, Angus. Bring all you get to me."

"Sure," Billy replied, with no great enthusiasm.

"Now, Dad," the sheriff went on, turning to the bar. "What happened?"

Derham told his story at greater length with more attention to detail. Much to McCobb's thinly concealed annoyance, it proved favorable to Smith. While the old-timer was declaring vehemently and profanely that the Texan had been provoked, Burbury picked up and opened the dandy's hip flask. Ignoring the sheriff's obvious, if unspoken, disapproval, the burly man sniffed at the flask's neck.

"It don't smell like bourbon," Burbury stated, when Derham had stopped speaking. Pouring the remaining spots of liquid onto his palm, he held them for Smith and the sheriff to see. The small pool in his hand was colorless. He tested it with the tip of his tongue and went on, "It don't look nor taste like bourbon, neither. Water, maybe, but not bourbon. Want to try a lick, sheriff?"

"I'll take your word for it!" McCobb said coldly, and swung on his heel to face the trio of drummers. Indicating the largest of them, he asked, "How did you see it, mister?"

By the time the sheriff had interrogated two of the drummers, he knew there was no case against Smith. Nor did the third traveling salesman change the pattern. All of the trio corroborated the old hostler's statement that the Texan had gone out of his way to avoid trouble, in the face of vicious insults and threats. Even more damning to McCobb's hopes had been the fact that Hayward not only instigated the fight but tried to take an unfair advantage. The drummers also verified that Hardy had drawn before the dandy was shot and so menaced Smith's life to such an extent that the Texan had been justified in shooting him.

During the giving of evidence, Billy had brought the third dead man's belongings to his uncle. They did not prove any more informative than the items found on Hardy or Hayward. Telling his nephew to have the bodies removed to the barn, the sheriff turned back to the Texan.

"Can I have a word with you, S—Mr. Smith?"

"It's your county, sheriff."

"In private," McCobb hinted, looking pointedly at Burbury.

"Mind if I hear what's said, Wax?" the burly man asked.

"*I* mind!" McCobb yelped.

"*I* don't," Smith drawled. "And I'm allowed to have a witness anytime I'm talking to a lawman. You'll know Supreme Court Ruling Eleven, Decision Twenty-Three, Clause Sixty-One, I reckon, sheriff?"

"Er, yes. Of course I know it," McCobb replied.

He did not, but felt sure that a man like Waxahachie Smith

would be fully conversant with any ruling or decision which gave him an advantage when dealing with an officer of the law. Already the Supreme Court had earned a reputation among peace officers for producing rulings which made their work more difficult. So McCobb did not doubt that Smith was within his legal rights to have Burbury present.

For his part, Smith wondered why he had agreed to Burbury's request. Sure, he was grateful to the burly man for saving his life, but he felt that Burbury was taking a whole heap too much interest in his doings. However, the decision had been made and there was no going back on it.

"Set up drinks for these three gents, barkeep," Burbury instructed, indicating the drummers who, having given their evidence, were eyeing Lily Shivers with interest. "They'll need it while they're helping tote the bodies out of here."

"Huh?" grunted the largest drummer.

"You was playing with them two," Burbury pointed out. "And they've got to be moved. Sheriff can deputize you to do it."

"So I can," McCobb agreed, looking his most pompous. "And I'm doing it."

"Man can get jailed for refusing due and lawful deputization by a sworn officer of the county," Smith warned as the drummers seemed on the verge of protesting. "Sheriff'd be in his legal rights to do that, too."

Muttering to themselves, the trio accepted McCobb's orders that they should help remove the bodies. With that matter under control, the sheriff suggested that he, Smith and Burbury should conduct their business away from the bar.

"It looks better," McCobb explained. "Let's go sit at the big table."

Before following Smith and the sheriff, Burbury picked up the first of the tops with which he had experimented. Dropping it into his right side pocket, he put its mate into the left. Then he walked after the two men in the direction of the big table.

"Don't get up, Miss Shivers," McCobb requested as the blonde made as if to rise. "We'll go down the other end."

Smith thought that he could detect a cynical smile as the blonde lowered her rump back to the seat. Slowly her eyes lifted to his, then ran over him from top to bottom. There was interest in her gaze, and not just caused by hands. Further thoughts on that subject ended as McCobb coughed twice, cleared his throat loudly and started speaking.

"I'm satisfied that you acted in self-defense, S—Mr. Smith. You're sure you don't know why they picked on you?"

"Nary a notion," the Texan replied.

"Or who could have hired them?"

"Nope. I've got a few enemies who might have, but none of them are up this ways far as I know."

"Where are you headed for?"

"Widow's Creek. I'll be going in the morning."

"Who're you—?" McCobb began, showing his relief at the news. Hurriedly revising his question, he continued, "Why're you going there?"

"For the county fair," Smith answered, eyeing the sheriff in a challenging manner. "Why else?"

McCobb let the query pass. If Smith carried out his declaration, he would go out of the sheriff's jurisdiction. Never a man to make work for himself, McCobb decided to let the whole affair slide.

"Like I said," he announced. "I'm satisfied you was forced into fighting. Most likely that young cuss figured to get a name as the man who gunned down Waxahachie Smith."

"Most likely," Burbury put in dryly.

"That being the case," the sheriff went on, "we'll say no more about it."

"Hardly seemed worthwhile fetching us from the bar," Burbury commented as McCobb crossed to where Gilpin was talking to the farmer. "Anyways, we'd've had to come here. Lily was saying's how she'd admire to meet you."

5

Worthy of His Hire

"So you're Waxahachie Smith," Lily Shivers said, after Burbury had performed the introductions. "I thought that Ric was joshing me when he told me your name."

Seen up close, the blonde was even more beautiful than from a distance. She met Smith's gaze with an air of equality. Accepting that she possessed considerable charm for members of the opposite sex, she did not try to play on it. There was an attitude of calm competence about her, as if she felt certain that she could match up to any man on his own terms and handle whatever play he chose to make.

"I'll go fetch us some drinks," Burbury announced, avoiding the question that Smith was preparing to fire at him. "Don't reckon this place'll run to wine, Lily."

"Whiskey'll do," the blonde replied, keeping her eyes on Smith. There was neither promise nor invitation in them, only a cool appraisal. "This's a mite north of your home range, Waxahachie."

"Man likes to see new places, ma'am," the Texan answered. "And you'd likely find 'Wax' comes easier to your tongue."

"I'll try, if you'll say 'Lily' instead of 'ma'am,'" the blonde promised, then she stopped smiling. "That was a trap if ever I saw one, Wax. Why'd they come gunning for you?"

"Somebody hired 'em. But I couldn't start to guess who."

"Maybe it's somebody who doesn't want you to get to Widow's Creek. I heard you tell McCobb that's where you're headed."

"And I am."

"For the county fair?"

"Why else?"

"So play cagey," Lily sniffed. "Could be I can help you. I've seen those three up at the Creek. They came in the day before I left for Cheyenne."

"Did, huh?" Smith said noncommittally. "Who'd they meet?"

"You think maybe I trailed them around?" Lily replied. "They were together in my place, but nobody joined them. And I saw the gambling man coming out of the side door of the bank."

"Side door?" Smith repeated.

"Wil's private-office door," the blonde elaborated. "He'd likely been in there talking business. With Wil, it'd have to be business."

Thinking back to Derham's comments about Lily not getting on with Wil Jeffreys, Smith wondered if he should mention his employer's identity. While the discovery might jolt the blonde into some enlightening comment, it could also have the opposite effect. Then all he would have achieved would have been to let Lily know that a rival—enemy, even—was going to hire him. Smith decided that he would lose more than he might gain by taking her into his confidence. So he was not sorry to see Burbury returning with a tray of drinks.

"Here we are," the burly man boomed, setting down the tray and handing one of its drinks to Lily.

"Just how long have you known who I am, Ric?" Smith challenged as Burbury sat down beyond the blonde.

"Would you believe me if I said only since the old-timer named you?"

"Not 'specially."

"He let on about it down to the barn. Come in while I was unhitching my rig."

"I figured you knew something," Smith declared. "You didn't mention about me wearing my gloves while I was eating."

"Hey, fellers," Lily put in. "I'm still sat here. At least throw me a smile now and then. It's bad for my reputation if I'm ignored."

"Sorry, Lily," Burbury grinned. "I reckon Wax's a mite uneasy in his mind over what happened. And so am I. Those fellers were sure set on seeing him dead. Way I see it, they was using that put-and-take game so's they'd have an excuse for doing it."

"By having that flashy-dressed yack call him down when he wouldn't play?" Lily asked. "He didn't first time Wax said no."

"Likely they wasn't sure where I sat in the game," Burbury replied. "I raked at Hayward, but he took it. Wasn't 'til I'd come over to you that it happened."

"What if Wax'd played the next time he was asked?"

"He'd already said 'no' once. So if he'd come in on that pot and took it, the other fellers in the game would've objected and given Hayward his chance," Burbury answered, and took the top from his left side pocket. Turning it over on the palm of his left hand, he examined it. "I dunno if it means anything, but some of the edges are rounder than the others."

"That's so it'll fall the right way, if you know the gaff," Lily explained. "The top tends to roll off the sides with the rounded edges and stop on those which are sharp."

"What's the gaff?" Smith inquired, knowing the word to be a gambler's expression for the secret which caused a crooked device to perform its dishonest function.

"If you spin it clockwise, which comes natural to a right-handed feller," the blonde explained, taking the top and demonstrating, "it lands on a 'put.' Turn it the other way and you get a 'take' every time. I had a jasper from a crooked gambling supply house 'round trying to sell me some gaffed and straight tops a few weeks back."

The drummers returned, cursing the weather and their lousy luck in being caught for such a stinking chore. Looking around, Smith found that the farmer and his wife had disappeared. Gilpin stood at the bar with the sheriff, while a couple of hostlers swabbed the blood from the floor. After throwing scowls at the Texan and Burbury, the drummers slouched across to the bar.

"Hardy was spinning counterclockwise all the time," Burbury reminded Smith.

"That'd be so nobody'd be able to complain he'd changed his way when he used the gaffed top," Lily guessed.

"Only he didn't get 'round to using it," Smith pointed out.

"Could be he was counting on you taking his offer, hitting a 'Put All' and not wanting to pay," Burbury suggested. "That'd've given Hayward a chance to call you down."

"Know what I think?" Lily asked. "I'm betting that Hardy hadn't meant to have Hayward take you until he'd won the pot. Then he got a signal from that other feller to do it. Or he fumbled while he was trying to switch tops and thought he'd made the marks suspicious, so he might's well get it over with. Hayward had already established that he wouldn't let anybody disrespect Hardy. So nobody'd think too much about him calling you over refusing what looked like a friendly offer."

"We'll never know for sure which it was," Smith predicted, and looked at Burbury. "How'd you figure that Moxley *hombre* was tied in with 'em?"

"That didn't take much doing," the burly man countered. "They'd all got the same kind of mud on their boots, for one thing."

"Moxley looked primed for trouble when he come in," Lily went on. "He'd been wearing a slicker, but took it off before he came through the door."

"In the barn, or wherever he left his hoss," Burbury corrected. "That didn't mean much. Feller with a price on his head likes to have a clear grab at his gun when he walks into a room full of strangers. Somebody among 'em might recognize him."

"*Somebody* did," Smith stated, staring pointedly at the burly man.

"Us traveling men from Schuyler, Hartley and Graham get around," Burbury answered blandly. "And I've always been real good at remembering faces."

"You're real good at handling a gun, too," Smith complimented.

"Man totes a wad of folding money like I do, he needs to be," Burbury answered. "Talking of guns, I'd admire to see yours."

Although Smith sensed that Burbury was deliberately changing the subject, he did not argue. He owed the burly drummer his life, so figured that he could put up with the other's reticence and evasions. In fact, Burbury could be speaking the truth and might be no more than he claimed, with a valid reason for knowing how to handle a gun.

"You mean how does a feller like me shoot it," Smith drawled.

"No offense, Wax," Burbury said, sounding sincere.

"None took," the Texan assured him, lifting out the Colt and placing it on the table. "Here, take a look."

At first glance, the revolver—with its metal parts the deep blue of the Best Citizen's Finish—might have passed for an ordinary Civilian Model Peacemaker. Closer observation revealed certain alterations. There was neither foresight nor trigger. The spur had been reduced in size, its checkering removed to leave it smooth and was fitted halfway down the curve of the hammer instead of at the top.

"It's a slip gun, isn't it?" Lily asked, studying the weapon. "I've heard of them, but the only one I ever saw just had its trigger tied back. Feller who used it fanned the hammer. He sure made a life-like corpse."

"Most folks who fan regular get that way," Smith admitted. "Which's why I had this old plow handle fitted up special."

"How?" Burbury inquired, and his interest had a genuine ring to it.

"Had the trigger and its half of the bolt spring left off. That lil stud on the hammer, what they call the bolt cam, 's only half the regular size. Throws less strain on the bolt arm and makes it work smoother. That short, slick spur's set low on the hammer so's I can thumb it back easier and the butt's maybe an inch shorter to give me a better grip."

"You must have put some thought into getting it right," Lily praised.

"Man with only one trade has to get the right tools, regardless," Smith answered. "Handling guns was just about the only thing I knew."

Looking at the tanned, expressionless face, Lily sensed something of the long, hard struggle Smith had made to face life after the accident that had cost him both forefingers. Only vague rumors circulated about how the loss had occurred. What she did know was that Smith's name had been prominent among Texas Rangers and he was said likely to become the youngest captain of that fabled law-enforcement body. Receiving what would have been regarded as a completely incapacitating injury had blasted his chances. Many men would have turned their back on guns and gunfighting, but Smith did not. She wondered what deep, driving compulsion had helped him to overcome the handicap and develop such a deadly technique and a weapon so perfectly adapted to his needs.

Waxahachie Smith interested Lily for a number of reasons.

"See you had the foresight took off to stop it catching on anything when you make that high cavalry twist-hand draw," Burbury commented, taking up the Colt for a closer inspection. "You wouldn't need it, anyways. They do say a slip gun's only good for short-range shooting." He glanced into the muzzle, stiffened and took a longer, more searching look down the tube. "Hey! The barrel's not rifled."

"Like you said," Smith replied, retrieving the revolver and returning it to his holster. "A slip gun's not much use over a distance. So I figured to give it a mite more range. I use three balls to a bullet, 'stead of one."

"Three!" Lily exclaimed.

"What they call a multiball cartridge," Smith elaborated. "Feller called Captain Wright designed them for the Army back in seventy-nine and I figured they'd be what I needed."

Coming through the front door, looking disconsolate and close to nausea, the McCobb brothers slouched without a glance at Smith across to the sheriff. After listening to what they had to say, McCobb walked over to the big table.

"Their hosses are down at the barn," the sheriff told Lily and her companions. "Moxley's slicker was on his saddle, but there wasn't nothing in their gear to help us."

"Wasn't, huh?" Burbury grunted.

"No," McCobb replied. "I didn't think there would be, but a peace officer has to make sure."

"Ain't that the living truth?" Burbury agreed solemnly, then he yawned and stretched. "Now me, I'm fixing to go to bed."

"Had they unsaddled, sheriff?" Smith inquired.

"Not none of 'em," McCobb answered. "You don't expect that kind to care for their hosses, do you?"

"Likely not," Smith admitted. "I reckon I'll be turning in, too. There's a long day's ride ahead of me comes morning."

"I'm going, comes to that," Lily declared. "If I stay out here, I'll have those drummers and—such—swarming all over me. It's bad enough I have to 'dovetail' all day with 'em, without being with them all night."

"I'll leave you to it, then," McCobb announced.

"I get the feeling you don't like peace officers, Ric," Smith commented as the sheriff ambled back to the bar.

"I don't like *some* peace officers," Burbury answered. "And them's're put in as political office-fillers're some of the some I don't like."

"Quastel over to Fremont County's one of the *some,*" Lily remarked. "Are you headed for Widow's Creek, Ric?"

"Sure. A county fair's a good place for a selling man to be. Folks have cash money in their pockets and're just itching to spend it."

"Just happen I want to buy something, Ric," Smith said. "What sort of doodads're you selling?"

"If it's in the company's dream book, I sell it," Burbury replied. "Well, I'll be saying good night."

"That's the first salesman I ever saw who didn't try to sell something given half a chance," Lily commented, watching Burbury head toward the men's sleeping quarters. "And was he fast, Wax. Real fast."

"Might not be a drummer, huh?" Smith said.

"I didn't say that," Lily countered. "Good night, Wax. I'll likely see you in the morning, but if I don't, drop by the Happy Bull for a drink—after the stage gets in."

While Lily glided off toward the women's room, Smith followed Burbury. On entering, he found that the farmer was already in bed. The little undertaker stood by another bed removing his jacket.

"If you gents're going out back," the small man said, "you'd best ask the stationmaster for a new dream book. I used the last page and the covers'd be rough on the butt end."

The reference to the dream book explained how the undertaker came to be in the building, although he had not passed through the barroom. If he had been using the privy, he could have entered the sleeping quarters by the back door.

"Thanks for telling me," Burbury grinned. "I was just going."

"Rain's stopped," the undertaker remarked to Smith as Burbury returned to the barroom.

"That's something to be thankful for," the Texan replied, realizing he had been so fully occupied all evening that he had been unaware of the aching which usually accompanied wet weather.

"Gilpin's gone to tell the dudes they don't need to be scared anymore," Burbury announced, returning with a newspaper in his hand. "This's the best old Dad in there could do."

"If it's a two-holer, I'll come with you," Smith offered. "I have to go and there might not be any paper."

"A *two*-holer?" Burbury grinned. "It's a *six*-holer. The pride of Sweetwater County, I've been told."

"May I have a private word with you, Mr. Smith?" the undertaker asked. "On a matter of some importance, for your ears alone."

"I reckon so," the Texan agreed. "You'd best go on ahead, Ric."

"Sure," the drummer replied. "I've near on waited too long now."

Letting Burbury get out of the back door, the little man stared at the farmer and made sure that he was asleep. Crossing to Smith's side, he dropped his voice in a secretive, almost furtive manner.

"I have something which might be of use to you."

"Such as?" Smith asked.

"Not so loud, I beg of you, sir," the undertaker hissed. "It is a sheet of paper I found in the third man's pocket."

"I thought you was supposed to be helping the sheriff," Smith said dryly, but held his voice to little higher than a whisper.

"In the Good Book, sir, we are told that the laborer is worthy of his hire. So I assume that I, Otis M. Capey, being a professional gentleman, should be even more so."

"Get to the white meat."

"Of course, sir. When I broached the subject of payment for my professional services, I was made certain that none would be forthcoming. So I considered myself ethically entitled to look out for your interests."

"And your own," Smith drawled. "Sure, I know. The laborer is worthy of his hire. Well, let's see what you've got."

"Just a sheet of paper," Capey replied, taking it from his left hip pocket but not holding it out. "With a message on it—but we haven't spoken of my hire."

"I haven't heard anything that's worth money," Smith pointed out.

"The message reads, 'Smith on his way from Laramie. Stop him getting here.'"

"Is *that* all?" Smith sniffed. "I know somebody sent them after me."

"There is something more, sir," Capey promised, still not offering the paper to. the Texan. "A name. But it would not be good business to proceed further until money has been discussed."

"Twenty dollars," Smith suggested, showing none of the interest he felt. If the message should be genuine, it proved that somebody in Widow's Creek had hired the three men.

"Twen—!" Capey began.

"That's a fair price and I'm too tired to bargain. 'Specially when all I have to do is call in the sheriff, tell him and see what you've got for free."

"I could destroy the paper before he came," the undertaker blustered.

"Not with me this close," Smith pointed out. "And if you did, you'd be in bad trouble. Maybe you don't know, but Article Eleven, Section Twenty-Three, Clause Sixty-One of the Wyoming Territorial Penal Code, Withholding Information from a Duly Sworn Peace Officer, says you can get five years in the pokey for doing it. Double if you attempt to, or destroy, said evidence."

"I don't share your legal knowledge, Mr. Smith," Capey confessed. "But there is small need for unpleasantness. We are both businessmen. I accept your offer and, as evidence of my good faith, here is the document."

"Gracias," Smith said, taking out his wallet and exchanging two of its ten dollar bills for the piece of folded paper.

On opening it out, Smith found it to be a page torn from a notebook. Wanting a better view of his purchase, he took it under the small lamp which hung in the center of the room. He did not doubt that the message would be as Capey had claimed, but wanted to check on other details. Although printed in block letters, Smith concluded that it had been written by a hand used to holding a pencil. The slight irregularities in the otherwise neat writing could have been to disguise it, or been caused by it being written in a hurry.

"I took the opportunity of examining it in the barn, sir," Capey commented quietly from Smith's side. "A businessman must be aware of his wares' value. There were slight scratches on the bottom of the paper. So I used my pencil and brought them into view."

Smith was already looking at the marks left in the blackened area at the foot of the page. Somebody had been writing on the sheet which had been above the one he held in the book. By rubbing a lead pencil gently over the area, the undertaker had exposed the two words that pressure had imprinted upon it.

"Well, sir," Capey breathed. "Have I been worthy of my hire?"

"I don't want the twenty simoleons back, if that's what you mean," Smith replied, folding the letter. To himself, he continued, "Who the hell, or what the hell, is Poona Woodstole?"

6

A Lady of Talent
and Integrity

"Dad! Dad Derham!" Waxahachie Smith roared, his voice throbbing with rage.

"What's up?" asked the old hostler, hurrying into the barn.

"Look at this!" the Texan commanded, furiously shaking two connected leather straps in his clenched left fist.

Even before he reached the burro, Derham recognized the things in Smith's hand for what they were. Coming up, he saw that the right girths—with the spacer still fitted between them—had been cut off just below the saddle's girth rings. Looking over, he found that the left side girths had been treated in the same manner. Smith's bedroll lay on the floor, the Colt New Lightning rifle leaning on it.

"What—!" the old-timer spluttered. "Who did it?"

"How the hell would I know?" Smith spat out savagely. "But if I find out, I'll shove my fingers up his nose and poke his eyes out from the inside. Where are those *hombres* who're supposed to sleep in here?"

"Hey!" protested a sleepy voice. "What's all the noise about?"

Still gripping the severed reins, Smith glared at the tall, gangling man who emerged from the rear of the barn. A second man followed him, coming from the small room, clad in undershirt, jeans and barefooted. Each showed signs of having been awoken from sleep. At the sight of Smith bearing down on them, the first man made as if to pick up a pitchfork which leaned against a stall.

"Leave it be, Seth, if you know what's good for you," Derham warned. "This here's Waxahachie Smith and he's got good cause to be riled."

Jerking his hand away from the pitchfork, the man stared at Smith. Behind Seth, the second hostler lost all his aggressive air.

"Some son of a bitch cut my girths," Smith announced, holding them before the duo. "Was you pair in here all night?"

" 'Cepting when we was working," Seth answered. "Which was most of the time. We had the stage to get ready for tomorrow, stock to tend to—"

"Did anybody come in while you was here?" Smith interrupted.

"Them fellers toting in the dead'n's," Seth replied.

"And after them?" the Texan asked.

"Nobody's I saw. Me 'n' Joel had to clean up in the bar after our other chores. Then we had us a meal, come down here and went to bed."

"Who-all left the men's room last night, Mr. Smith?" Derham inquired.

"Near on everybody, I reckon," Smith replied bitterly, walking back to the burro.

By going to the privy as soon as Burbury had come back, Smith had kept the undertaker's information to himself. In fact, the burly drummer had shown no interest in the matter and was already in bed when the Texan returned. After that, Smith had spent a somewhat disturbed and restless night. His natural caution had dictated that he should select a bed in a corner. Situated at the left side of the rear wall, he found his choice to have disadvantages. Always a light sleeper, he had been wakened every time one of the other travelers went out back. During the night, all the room's occupants, except Capey, had gone by his bed at one time or another.

At the time, Smith had regarded the departures and returns as nothing more than a nuisance which disturbed his rest. Looking down at the saddle, he could see that one of the men who went out might have had a motive other than relieving the call of nature.

"You'd best go see if I can get a place on the stage, Dad," Smith said, modifying his anger-filled voice as he realized that he could not hold the hostler responsible for his misfortune. "I'll ride up in it, with my horse tied to the back."

"Sure thing, Mr. Smith," Derham answered, and scuttled away.

Footsteps came to the Texan's ears. He heard a rapid exchange of talk, without being able to make out more than the old-timer's cracked voice speaking hurriedly. A few seconds later, Burbury and the McCobbs entered.

"I hear you've had trouble, Mr. Smith," the sheriff greeted, a malicious glint of satisfaction warring with the worry in his eyes.

"There's some's'd call it that," the Texan agreed. "My girths've been cut."

"Cut?" repeated Billy, throwing a delighted grin at Angus.

"You reckon it's funny?" Smith demanded quietly.

"Go tend to the horses, you pair!" McCobb snapped at his nephews, then turned to the Texan. "Them three fellers who tried to kill you must've done it afore they come looking for you."

"Sure," Burbury agreed. "They did it so you couldn't come after 'em after they'd killed you, Wax."

"Nobody else'd have reason to do it," McCobb protested. "Er, what do you intend to do now, Mr. Smith?"

"Take the stage to Widow's Creek, if I can get on it."

"How about your horse?" Burbury asked.

"Figured on taking him tied to the stage," Smith replied.

"They'll be pushing hard, changing teams every ten miles or so," Burbury warned. "Even without toting weight, your horse won't be in much of a condition time you get to the Creek."

"I don't want to take time to come back for him when I've got my saddle fixed," Smith pointed out.

"So I'll fetch him up for you," the drummer offered. "I'll not be traveling as fast as the coach, but I'll be there around noon tomorrow."

"Sounds like a smart notion to me," the sheriff remarked.

"And me," Smith drawled. "I'll be obliged if you'd do that, Ric."

There was nothing to be lost, and plenty to gain, by letting Burbury take the horse. No matter who, or what, the burly man might really be—and Smith felt certain he was no ordinary drummer—the Texan was sure he could be trusted to deliver the *bayo-lobo* to Widow's Creek. With the stagecoach stopping only long enough to change teams, Smith's mount would have time to rest and graze. So Burbury offered the best solution.

"There's a seat for you, Mr. Smith!" Derham announced, entering at a rapid walk. "Only you'll have to get there straightaway."

"I'll see to your horse, Wax," Burbury promised. "You get going."

"Lemme tote your rig," the old-timer offered.

Allowing the old-timer to carry his saddle, Smith gathered up his bedroll and rifle. They left the barn and went to where the stagecoach stood, its team hitched and passengers on board, outside the station building. Smith passed up his bedroll, then took and handed his saddle to the shotgun messenger. Waiting to make sure that the rig was laid on its side and not stood upon the skirts, Smith looked inside. The farmer, his wife and the two Eastern women occupied the rear seat. In front of them, the pair of dudes and Capey "dovetailed" with the drummers. Apparently the prospector had either reached the end of his journey or was waiting for another stagecoach, for Lily had nobody facing her on the center seat.

"Hey, Wax," the blonde greeted, looking through the window. "Are you coming on the stage?"

"Why, sure," the Texan replied, and opened the door. Rifle in hand, he swung inside and sat facing the girl. "I have to."

"Somebody steal your horse?" asked the largest drummer, sullenly watching Smith's right knee resting against the material of Lily's traveling costume.

"Why?" Smith answered, setting the butt of his rifle on the floor against the door. "Have you got it?"

"Mercy!" Lily put in. "I thought it was so you could be near me."

Disapproving clucks came from behind Smith, but the blonde ignored them. She smiled at him and he could feel the drummer at his side moving restlessly. Before any more could be said, or done, the driver cracked his whip and the stagecoach started moving. Burbury stood at the doors of the barn and raised a hand in a cheery wave as the vehicle went by. Leading out their horses, the sheriff and his nephews mounted and followed the stage.

Watching the range fall behind him, Smith thought about the damage to his saddle and why it had been inflicted. Then he turned his gaze to the interior of the coach. In all probability, the person who had cut the girths was riding with him. Smith doubted if the McCobb brothers had done it out of spite. Nor did the sheriff's theory hold water. Sure the three men had been sent to prevent Smith from reaching Widow's Creek. But they had intended to kill him, not merely delay him. So the knife had been used *after* their attempt had failed.

Not to stop him getting to Widow's Creek, though.

At best the damage would have only held him until he could have it repaired. No. The girths had been cut so that he would not arrive before the stagecoach could carry warning of his coming. So one of Smith's traveling companions must be the culprit. Unless it had been Burbury. Yet there seemed no logical reason for the burly man to have done it. If he had wished to prevent Smith's arrival, he would have let Moxley kill the Texan. Nor had the damage to the saddle caused Smith to arrive at the town later than Burbury, in the buggy, would reach it.

There was Lily Shivers to consider. Smith had no way of knowing whether she had left the station building during the night. If she suspected his employer's identity, she might have taken steps to make him arrive later than expected.

Thinking of the blonde led Smith to look more closely at her. She seemed to take pleasure in antagonizing the other female passengers. A conversation had started among the dudes and drummers, in which Lily took an active part. Witty, without being coarse, she kept the men amused and the women annoyed. Watching her, Smith sensed that it was the latter result she was aiming at.

On rolled the stagecoach, making good time over the well-worn trail. At the first relay station, the McCobbs took their departure, having reached the county's boundary line. Nobody seemed unduly alarmed after the peace officers had ridden off.

Another twenty miles and two changes of teams fell behind the travelers. Coming over a hill, the trail ran parallel to the southern bank of the Sweetwater River's Big Elk Fork. Across the stream, the land appeared to be of better quality than that flanking the trail.

"Looks like they got over the winter of 'eighty-six better across that side than over here," Smith remarked to Lily.

"Sure," agreed the blonde. "Mind you, Charlie Hopkirk and Poona Woodstole always showed better sense than most ranchers."

"How come?" Smith asked, ignoring Capey's pointed glance at the mention of the latter name.

"You maybe know how it was before 'eighty-six," Lily replied. "Ranchers were running every head they could—"

"And more," the biggest drummer interrupted. "They over-grazed the range."

"Not all of them," Lily contradicted. "And for sure not Charlie 'n' Poona. For a limey, Poona's a smart, cattle-knowing feller. So they ran their spread with what he called a long-term view in mind. Built up their herds with picked stock, instead of raising anything and everything. They developed their land, took care of the grazing. Maybe they didn't make so much money as the others, but they came out of the big die-off with cash in the bank and cattle carrying their brand. That side of the river's the best grazing land in the Territory."

"How about this side?" Smith inquired.

"You can see," growled the drummer. "It's the leavings, all that farmers ever get given."

"Time was they didn't want it," Smith pointed out.

"Times change," the drummer observed.

"Land doesn't, unless it's worked on," Lily pointed out. "Which this side of the river wasn't before 'eighty-six. Now farmers're moving in and finding they can't make eating money."

"Not *this* side of the river," the drummer agreed.

"Across it's C Lazy P land, with a clear title bought, worked for and earned," the blonde said coldly. "Nobody's got the right to homestead on it."

"And nobody's got the right to glom onto that much land," the drummer declared. "Only the big ranchers've done it and sure aim to hold onto what they've got."

"Meaning?" Smith asked quietly, knowing that the man's last sentence had been directed his way.

"Nothing," grunted the drummer. "Except maybe the big ranchers won't have it all their own way from now on."

"That's a strange-looking rifle, Wax," Lily remarked. "I've never seen one like it."

"It's a Colt New Lightning, Lily," the elder of the dudes informed her.

Allowing the man to explain the virtues of the ordinary production-line Colt New Lightning rifle, Smith digested the information he had just gathered. One of the possibilities he had considered as the cause of the urgent summons was trouble between ranchers and homesteaders.

Going by her comments, Lily tended to favor the ranchers. Maybe Mayor Jeffreys supported Governor Thomas Moonlight, a man known to be sympathetic to the cause—and, some said, the extra voting potential—of the homesteaders. That could be the cause of their animosity.

A question about the Colt rifle's capabilities as a hunting weapon took the Texan's attention from his train of thought. Nor did he find time to return to it, as the discussion lasted until the stagecoach arrived at Widow's Creek.

The Big Elk Fork split the town into two sections. Looking around him in the fading light, Smith decided that the stream served as a dividing line between the better-off and poorer sections of the community. That showed in the quality of the buildings, which was of a much higher standard north of the river. To the south lay the main business section, the stores, places of entertainment and homes of the working classes of the town. Capey and the drummers headed in that direction. Not unexpectedly, the dudes had their baggage carried over one of the bridges into the northern section.

When Smith had asked Lily's advice about obtaining accommodation, she suggested that he should use the Simple Hotel. In addition to offering good food and clean beds, it had the advantage, she claimed, of being close to her place. Somewhat to his surprise, after gathering a trio of loafers to carry her bags and his saddle and bedroll, Lily had led him across the stream.

Passing through a prosperous street given over to professional men's business premises and civic buildings, Lily pointed with pride to her saloon. Two floors high, solidly made of stone, the Happy Bull glowed with light and rang with the sounds of people enjoying themselves. Facing it across the street, dark and deserted, stood Jeffreys' Bank.

"I've got a new sign for out front that'll knock Wil—folks bow-legged," Lily remarked. "The hotel's just down there. If you have trouble getting a room, tell the clerk I sent you."

"Will that help?" Smith grinned.

"What I know about him, he'll not dare keep you out," the blonde chuckled. "After you've settled in, mind you come along for a drink."

"I'll be in after I've cleaned up and fed," Smith promised.

"You'll come and have supper with me," Lily corrected. "Unless you've got other arrangements—?"

"None that I know of," Smith assured her and, after she had disappeared into the saloon, walked on in the direction of the Simple Hotel.

Obtaining a room did not call for the power of Lily's name. Although remarking that the hotel was filling up, the desk clerk stated that Smith could have accommodation for as long as he cared to book it. Making his arrangements, the Texan went up to his quarters, paid off the man who had carried his gear and tipped the bellhop who had acted as their guide. Then he made ready for his visit to Lily's saloon.

Almost an hour later, washed, shaved and dressed in clean clothes, Smith walked into the Happy Bull. Its big main barroom was as elegant and well-equipped as any he had ever seen. Already a fair-sized crowd of customers was making use of its drinking or gambling facilities. Gaily-dressed girls moved among the cowhands, farmers, soldiers and townsmen while the saloon's male employees carried out their duties quietly, capably and in a friendly manner. Everything Smith saw told him that he was in a well-run place. What he had seen of Lily Shivers had made him expect to find it that way.

Crossing to the long, shining bar, Smith could see no sign of Lily. Then he grinned. It was *loco* to expect her to make an appearance so soon. She would take longer than a man to freshen up and change.

While waiting for Lily, Smith fell into conversation with a couple of prosperous-looking townsmen. He had left his jacket at the hotel, but the rest of his clothes hinted at his having money. Probably the pair took him for a Texas rancher and, as such, worth cultivating. From what they had to say, the man regarded Lily as a woman of ability and integrity. They also found considerable amusement in her flouting of conventions and made laughing comments about how she put a burr under the "good" women of the town's saddles with her behavior.

Half an hour went by before Lily made her entrance. When she did, it became obvious to Smith that the majority of her customers shared the townsmen's high opinion of her. Her hair had been tidied, face made up, and she wore a green satin dress which clung to her voluptuous body like a second skin as she came down the wide staircase from the first floor.

"What'd you bring back for us from the big city, Lily?" a man yelled.

"Why, *me*," the blonde answered. "What else?"

Excusing himself to the two townsmen, Smith walked toward the stairs. Another man intercepted Lily before Smith reached her. Tall, slim, wearing a well-cut brown suit, white shirt and red necktie, the man would be in his early twenties. His dark hair had been slicked down with bay rum, but now looked rumpled, while his handsome face carried an expression of mingled condescension and indignation.

"What's all this, Lily?" he demanded. "I've lost all my money playing blackjack and the dealer says he won't accept my IOU."

"That's right," the blonde answered calmly as she kept walking. "It's the house rule, Stanley."

Shooting out his right hand, the young man caught hold of Lily's left bicep as she went by. Anger flickered on the blonde's face. Clenching her right fist in a capable manner, she swung to face him.

"Just take your cotton-picking hand off the lady," Smith ordered.

Annoyance glinted on the young man's handsome face as he looked at the speaker. Clearly he considered himself to be a person of privilege and authority, who should not be addressed in such a manner by a stranger. Releasing Lily's arm, he stabbed his hand under the left side of his jacket.

"Who the hell do you think you're talk—?"

"Boy!" Smith cut in, barely louder than at a whisper. "Unless that hand comes straight out and empty, I'll draw on you. And I never fetch my gun out unless I'm fixing to kill the man who made me pull it."

A hush fell on the tables nearest to the scene and spread across the room. Smith stood with his gloved thumbs tucked into his waistband, eyes fixed firmly on Stanley's face. There was something in the Texan's gaze which made the young man look away.

"What's this, Lily?" Stanley hissed, bringing his empty right hand into view. "Have you started fetching in—"

"If you're fixing to say what I figure you are," Smith interrupted in the same flat, yet savage voice, "don't."

"If you want broke money, Stanley—" Lily began.

"I don't want, nor need, your charity!" the young man blazed, then spun on his heel and stamped out of the building.

"Who was that?" Smith inquired, as talk rose all around and the various activities of the customers resumed.

"Stanley Jeffreys," the blonde replied, a mocking smile twisting at her lips. "Our esteemed mayor's younger brother."

7

The Mayor of Widow's Creek

"Come this way, please, Mr. Smith," requested the lanky, miserable-featured bank teller with an air of solemn politeness.

The time was ten o'clock on the morning after Smith's arrival in Widow's Creek and he had come to interview his prospective employer.

After Stanley Jeffreys' departure, the Texan had spent an enjoyable evening at the Happy Bull saloon. Receiving no other introduction than "Mr. Wax Smith of Texas," he had been accepted by the other customers. In fact, he had been accorded their respect when it had become obvious that he was regarded favorably by Lily Shivers. Although he had heard plenty about the various sporting and social events proposed for the forthcoming county fair, he had received no hint of why the mayor might require his specialized services.

When Smith had suggested that Wil Jeffreys might come and complain about the disrespect shown to his younger brother, there had been much hilarity. He had been assured that the mayor would never think of entering a saloon. Wishing to avoid arousing Lily's suspicions, Smith had let the matter drop. Probably Jeffreys belonged to one of the religious sects which disapproved of drinking and other pleasures connected with saloons. Putting off further attempts at obtaining information about the mayor, Smith had settled down to enjoy himself.

Having spent a comfortable night at the Simple Hotel, Smith had risen late. He had breakfasted, made use of the hotel's barber shop and, neatly dressed and clean-shaven, set off to meet the mayor. Remembering that Wil Jeffreys was also the banker, he had called in at the bank. On seeing the telegraph message which had brought him to Wyoming, the teller had hurried into a room with "w.s.p. jeffreys. president" inscribed on its door.

Going through the gate in the front office's dividing rail, Smith wondered what kind of reception he would receive from the banker. If Brother Stanley had gone home tale-telling and described Lily's protector, Jeffreys would probably identify Smith as that man. In view of the enmity between the banker and Lily, he might even decide against hiring the Texan. In which case, Smith decided, he would be justified in retaining his advance payment.

Entering the bank president's spacious, comfortably furnished office, Smith found another reason, besides religious objections, why Wil Jeffreys would not go into a saloon. Looking across the large desk which faced the door, he flashed up his right hand to remove his hat.

"Well, Mr. Smith," said the mayor of Widow's Creek. "Now that you have seen me, do you object to being hired by a woman?"

Coal-black hair, taken back tight into an unattractive bun, could not wipe away the beauty of Wilhemina Jeffreys' face. She had schooled her classic features into a coldly serious expression, but they were tanned and glowed with health. An unadorned black Basque-waist jacket, as severe as a martinet Army officer's regulation tunic, a plain white blouse, and a black balmoral skirt fought to conceal the fact that feminine curves lay underneath them. Yet Smith sensed that the garments hid something most women would, secretly anyway, wish to possess; a figure as rich, full and voluptuous as Lily Shivers' gorgeous frame. Clean, strong hands devoid of jewelry and with the nails cut short rested on the top of the desk. Brown eyes looked from behind gold-rimmed spectacles, examining the Texan with as much interest as he studied her.

"Well," Wil Jeffreys went on, after a moment. "Do you?"

"Why should I?" Smith countered. "Do you print your own money?"

"I beg your pardon!" Wil said, snapping her gaze from his gloves to the bronzed, unsmiling face.

"Lady," Smith drawled. "As long as you pay in good ol' United

States dollars, I don't care whether it's a woman or a man who hires me."

Once more Wil's eyes flashed over Smith. There was nothing of a woman looking at a man in her scrutiny, any more than he found any sign of femininity in the office. While well and comfortably furnished, the room was clearly a place in which men conducted business. There were neither flowers on the desk nor dainty drapes at the windows; nothing to suggest that the mayor and bank president belonged to the weaker sex.

"Sit down, please," Wil said, and it came as an order despite the third word. Pushing across a cigar box, she went on, "You may smoke if you wish."

"Gracias," Smith replied, taking a cigar from the box and crackling it between his left thumb and second finger.

"You approve?" Wil inquired as he bit off the end of the cigar and lit it with the candle of the matchstick fastened to the box.

"It's a good cigar. My mother knew good tobacco and always used to pick cigars for pappy."

"But, disregarding my choice of cigars, you're surprised to find out I'm a woman?"

"Some," Smith admitted.

"You believe that a woman's place should be in the home?" Wil challenged.

"If I'd ever given thought to it," Smith drawled, "I'd say she'd know best where she should be. And what she's best suited to doing."

"That's male condescension."

"I thought it made good sense. If a woman can't cook, sew and tend to a wife's chores, she'd be better off out of the home."

Stiffening on her hard, straight-backed chair, Wil sucked in a deep breath. She took off her glasses, glared at Smith and said, "I'm a very good cook and I make or mend my clothes when the need arises, quite adequately too."

"I'm not gainsaying it, ma'am," the Texan replied.

"Let's get down to business!" Wil suggested haughtily. "I understand that you are an experienced peace officer, loyal to your employers, tactful and capable."

"I couldn't've put it better myself."

"These are facts, Mr. Smith, not compliments. You also have a reputation for direct action, considerable skill in handling weapons and people—and no exaggerated ideas of the sanctity of human life."

"If that means I'm willing to kill anybody who looks like he aims to kill me, it's a fact, not a compliment," Smith answered. "Maybe you'd best tell me what I'm here for."

"Does it matter?" Wil asked, laying her spectacles on the desk. "I thought you would take any work if the price was right."

"Only if it doesn't involve heavy toting—and's legal 'n' honest."

"That pays you back for riling me about a woman's place," Wil smiled.

That smile changed her own face and showed its full beauty. Then it went as quickly as it had come, leaving the cold, impassive mask.

"The work is legal and honest, although it may involve you in heavy toting, carrying drunks to jail. I want to employ you as part of the town's special police force during the week of the county fair."

"You don't have any law of your own?"

"We do," Wil admitted, a touch defiantly. "And I may say that, under normal conditions, our marshal runs an efficient office."

"Then why—?"

"Do you object to taking his place?"

"Lady. For what you're going to pay me, I don't give a damn about it."

"But you're still curious," Wil insisted.

"A mite," Smith conceded.

"I feel that the local officers would not be able to enforce the law adequately during the fair because they are just that, local men with homes and *friends* in Widow's Creek," Wil enlarged. "So I have arranged that they be sent on vacation and am bringing in men with no local connections—or friends—to run the law for the week. Does that clarify the situation?"

"Well enough," Smith admitted, seeing the lady mayor's reasons more clearly and wondering if the town marshal had an equal understanding of her motives. "You-all said I'd be *part* of a special police force. Who're the rest of it?"

There was a knock at the door on the left side of the room, presumably the one from which Lily had seen Hardy emerging. Excusing herself, Wil rose and went to open it. She admitted a tall, handsome man about Smith's age. Dressed like a successful professional gambler, he wore a silver-concha-decorated gun belt with a pearl-handled Colt Civilian Peacemaker in a low-hanging Missouri Skintite holster.

"I've sent for five good men, Mr. Smith," Wil stated, and indicated the newcomer. "This is Talbot Ottaway, the first of them to arrive."

"Howdy, Wax," Ottaway greeted, white teeth gleaming in a smile which did not reach his eyes. "Long time no see."

"Could be I've always seen you first, *Mister* Ottaway," Smith replied, remaining seated and ignoring the other's extended right hand.

"I believe that you both left the Texas Rangers about the same time," Wil remarked as she returned to her seat.

"Same time, different reasons," Smith replied. "I left with a clean record."

There was no doubting the animosity of the two men. Ottaway's smile faded and he darted a glance at Wil, then swung his attention back to Smith.

"So did I!" Ottaway growled. "And *I* can go back to Texas if I want to."

"Gentlemen!" Wil snapped, slapping her left palm on the desk's top. "I'm not particularly interested in your pasts. Nor do I expect your previous differences of opinion to affect the services I'm buying. If I'm speaking too plainly, say so."

"You're talking good sense, W—Miss Jeffreys," Ottaway assured her, and Smith kept quiet.

"Very well," Wil said, without looking at the tall, seated Texan. "As he arrived first, I thought that Mr. Ottaway should act as marshal."

"Thanks for the cigar," Smith said, shoving back his chair ready to rise.

"You don't agree with my suggestion?" Wil inquired.

"I flat out refuse it," Smith stated, coming to his feet.

"Hell. There's no sense in stomping out in a tizz, Wax," Ottaway put in and dipped his right hand into his jacket's side pocket. "I'm game to take a chance if you are."

"What kind of a chance?" Smith asked cautiously, slipping off his right glove and staring pointedly at the other man's jacket pocket.

"We'll flip a coin for it," Ottaway suggested, producing a nickel and balancing it on his thumb and forefinger. "Call it, Wax. If you win, you're marshal."

"How do you feel about it, Miss Jeffreys?" Smith inquired.

"Go ahead, if it will settle things," Wil authorized.

Propelled by Ottaway's thumb, the coin flipped spinning into the air. Smith waited until it reached the apex of its flight, then called, "Tails!"

A flicker of annoyance crossed Ottaway's face. Stabbing out his right hand, he caught the coin and dropped it, without looking at it, into his pocket. Once more the friendly, mouth-only smile came to his face.

"I only said it to see if you'd take a chance, Wax," the man announced and looked at Wil. "Anyways, ma'am, it wouldn't be right for me to be over him. He was a sergeant in the Rangers and I never made higher than private."

"And there's nothing but 'tails' on that nickel," Smith went on.

"Huh?" Wil gasped, showing emotion for the second time since the Texan had entered the office.

"It's an old trick, ma'am," Smith continued. "He makes the offer and spins the coin, counting on me doing like maybe ninety-nine folks out of a hundred and saying 'heads.' When I didn't, he caught it and made out he'd only been funning."

"Is that true, Mr. Ottaway?" Wil demanded.

For several seconds, Ottaway did not reply. Hatred showed on his face, although only an experienced reader of human emotions might have detected it. Smith had the necessary experience. So he stood with a relaxed attitude which did not fool the other man. There was an unspoken, open challenge in the Texan's demeanor all too plain to anybody who knew Waxahachie Smith—and Ottaway had bitter reason to know him. It had been Smith's findings which caused Ottaway to be "requested" to hand in his resignation from the Texas Rangers. If the Fuentes brothers had not intervened, Ottaway knew that the resignation would have been a dismissal and probably worse.

Ottaway faced a difficult decision. To answer in the negative would amount to calling Smith a liar. There was only one reply to that. Looking at Smith's bare right hand, Ottaway recalled the speed with which it could once draw and shoot a Colt. Nor had Smith lost his skill, if all the rumors making the rounds be true. Sucking in a breath, Ottaway reached a decision. Forcing an ingratiating smile to his lips, he nodded his head.

"Sure. Only it's not such an old trick. Seeing's Wax caught me out good and square, I'm willing to work under him. You're smarter than I thought, Wax."

"You're not, Mr. Ottaway," Smith replied and sat down, but he did not replace the glove. "Who're the other fellers you've asked, ma'am?"

"Frank Straw—" Wil began.

"He won't be coming," Smith commented. "Didn't you know that he'd took lead in that railroad fuss over to Kansas?"

"No!" Wil admitted.

"Wasn't you in that same fuss, Mr. Ottaway?" Smith challenged.

"Frank must've got his after I'd pulled out," Ottaway replied. "And I don't recall hearing about it happening."

"Then Mr. Straw won't be here," Wil said, eyeing Ottaway in a coldly calculating manner. "The other two are C. B. Frith, who has wired his confirmation, and Seaborn Tragg."

"I've never had dealings with Frith," Smith remarked. "But Seaborn Tragg's married up and gone to live peaceable down to Rockabye County, Texas."

"So old Seaborn's give up being a tin-star, has he," Ottaway put in with false joviality. "I'd've thought being a John Law runs in the Tragg family's blood."*

"The question is," Wil said, ignoring the comment, "do you gentlemen think that three of you can handle the work, or shall I try to bring in more men?"

"I don't see that it'll need so all-fired many more," Smith declared. "The town's not Dodge City, nor even Laramie as far's size goes. Against that, you've laid on races for horses, chuck wagons and fellers on foot. There's roping contests and a prizefight among the things that'll bring in the cheaters and sharks. On top of them, you'll have the town packed with visitors all aiming to have a good time. There'll be work in plenty, but three of us ought to be able to handle it. What do you reckon, Ottaway?"

"Being a man who likes to sleep now and then, I'd go for two or three more," Ottaway replied. "Let's not forget Governor Moonlight and some important folk're coming. They need careful watching."

"That's true," Wil admitted. "In addition to the Governor, Mr. Smith, there will be members of the Congressional Committee which is examining Wyoming's request to be made a state. If they see the fair carried off peacefully and without trouble, it will be a big point in our favor."

Before any more could be said, the door through which Smith had entered the office was opened.

"Hey, sis," greeted Stanley Jeffreys, strolling in. "I heard Tal Otta—" He slammed to a halt, the words trailing away as he caught sight of Smith. Stabbing his left forefinger in the Texan's direction, he demanded, "What's this jasper doing here?"

"Mr. Smith is one of the men I've brought in to keep the peace during the fair," Wil answered, her chilly tone showing that she disapproved of the intrusion.

"You know him from someplace, Stan?" Ottaway inquired.

"He was at the Happy Bull last night!" Jeffreys commenced.

"Make sure the rest of it's as truthful as that," Smith advised.

* The Tragg family still has "John Law" in its blood, as is told in the author's Rockabye County stories of the modern West.

"Well, Stanley?" Wil demanded when her brother showed a re-luctance to continue with his statement.

"Seems strange, way you and her don't get along," Jeffreys fi-nally announced. "Him and Lily Shivers was acting real friendly."

"That's right enough, ma'am, 'cept it was more friendly than real," Smith confirmed. "One thing you should know. No matter whose pay I'm drawing, I pick my own friends."

"Even if the friends' interests clash with those of your em-ployer?" Wil asked, eyes even with the Texan's.

"If they do, I change my friends—or employers," Smith de-clared. "Only not necessarily in that order."

"It needn't come to that," Wil stated. "My feelings toward Li—Miss Shivers are personal and involve only the two of us. Did you want to see me, Stanley?"

"Like I told you," Jeffreys answered, "old Ryall said that Tal was in here. So I came in to ask him when he's going to let me win the five dollars back that he took from me pitching horseshoes yesterday."

"We won't be long," Wil told him.

Listening to her, Smith formed the impression that she did not approve of her brother's friendship with Ottaway. That might be caused by nothing more than snobbery, but he felt that Wil showed right good sense. From what he had seen of Jeffreys, Smith doubted if the young man approached the lady banker in the mat-ter of intelligence. Let a self-opinionated yack like him keep com-pany with a man of Ottaway's kind and he would be liable to wind up in bad trouble. Smith figured it was none of his affair and kept the thoughts to himself.

"Well, gentlemen," Wil went on. "I would like to reach a deci-sion as the fair starts on Monday. We only have five days left. Do we need extra men?"

"I've been around town longer than you, Wax," Ottaway re-marked. "And I say we do."

"I'm listening," Smith replied.

"So far there's been no trouble around here between the farmers and ranchers. But some of 'em are fixing to homestead north of the Big Elk Fork. While Moonlight's down here'd be a good chance for the nesters to rile up the cowhands. Then the Grange can start screeching about what bad *hombres* the ranchers are."

"That's one of the reasons I tried to hire you five gentlemen," Wil admitted. "Poona Woodstole and Charlie Hopkirk won't sit back and let homesteaders take the land they've developed and paid for. So, if nesters cross the Fork, there'll be trouble which won't stay outside town."

"Likely," Smith agreed. "Only I don't see how we can stop it happening."

"I've called a meeting between the ranchers and the head of the Grange in this area. They're all reasonable men and know what's at stake. It's the hotheads and agitators we have to watch for. Not on the range, but in town, stirring up bad feelings. That's where you come in. I'm counting on you to keep things peaceable."

"Where do the extra men come from?" Smith asked.

"I hoped that you—and Mr. Ottaway—could help me hire them."

"Won't your local officers give up their vacations and help?"

"No, Mr. Smith," Wil replied and, for a moment, she looked embarrassed. "It's been suggested, but they—"

"Don't cotton to the notion of working with hired guns," Smith finished for her when the words tailed off. "Can't say's how I blame them for it, ma'am. I don't myself."

"Can you help raise the men?" Wil insisted.

"There's not a heap of time for us to gather 'em," Smith pointed out and, on an impulse, continued, "I might be able to raise one man, though."

"Do I know him?" Ottaway asked.

"How would I know who you know?" Smith countered. "Thing being, *I* know him."

"That's a good recommendation," Jeffreys sniffed, "going by the quality of some of your friends."

"That's enough, Stanley!" Wil snapped.

"Boys' got something stuck in his craw, it's better out," Smith drawled, eyeing Jeffreys with cold disdain. "Could be, if I met 'em, I'd not reckon much to *his* choice of friends. And, you rile me too much, I'm liable to tell your sister just how we met at the Happy Bull."

"All right, Wax," Ottaway drawled as Jeffreys relapsed into a sulky silence. "We'll count your *amigo* in. Come on, Stan. Let's you and me go around town to see if anybody's come in who's worth hiring. We'll let you see 'em first, Miss Jeffreys."

"Sure," Jeffreys agreed. "I might even take the job myself. Let's go."

Watching Wil's lips tighten, Smith knew that he had read her earlier emotions correctly. Yet, although she clearly disapproved of her brother's association with Ottaway, she made no attempt to stop him leaving with the other man. Letting out a low sigh as the door closed, the girl turned a masklike face to the Texan.

"When can you start, Mr. Smith?"

"As soon as we've talked about money,"

"One hundred dollars on top of the two hundred I've already advanced for the week. Your accommodation, ammunition and reasonable expenses covered by the town. If you take any wanted men, the reward money goes whichever way you and the other officers decide to deal with it."

"Sounds reasonable," Smith admitted. "How much do I get for working the rest of this week?"

"Another hundred and the same terms," Wil offered.

"You've just hired a man," Smith declared.

"And this friend of yours?" Wil wanted to know.

"I reckon he'll come in," Smith replied with a grin. "He reckons to be a pretty good salesman."

"I'll not ask what that means," Wil decided, without smiling. Opening the top drawer of her desk, she took out a marshal's badge and a bible. "If you're ready, I'll swear you in now."

"How about your regular marshal?"

"He agreed to start his vacation from the time I appointed a temporary successor."

Taking the badge, Smith pinned it on his vest's left breast. He tried to recall how many times he had performed such an act since taking up his new profession. With his right hand on the bible and left raised, he repeated the oath of office after Wil. One thing he knew for sure. No matter how she tried to hide it, he had never been sworn in by a prettier person. Not until the ceremony had ended did he realize that Wil had not put on her spectacles before reading the words for him to repeat.

"Excuse me, Miss Jeffreys," the teller said, poking his head around the door after knocking. "Mr. Hopkirk and Mr. Woodstole are waiting to see you."

"Ask them to come in," the girl replied. "Don't go, Mr. Smith. I would like you to meet these two gentlemen."

Smith nodded his agreement. That suggestion had saved him trying to invent an excuse to remain. He wanted to meet Poona Woodstole, whose name had been on a message carried by a man sent to kill him.

8

Faces from Smith's Past

In appearance, the two men who entered Wil's office could not have been different. First of them to come through the door was a short, leathery old Texas rancher. One of the breed who, in the depression-dark days following the War between the States, had helped Texas grow from hide and horn and reach prosperity,* and who, later, had seen the potential of the Wyoming rangelands which had been spurned by the homesteader to whom it had originally been offered.

Keen eyes twinkled in a seamed, oak-brown face. To show that he did not hold with newfangled contraptions, Charlie Hopkirk carried a cap-and-ball 1860 Army Colt in his holster. Smith did not regard it as a relic or a decoration.

Like his partner, Poona Woodstole wore the dress of a working cowhand. Tall, slim, good-looking, there was an air of neat, calm ability about him. Balancing the holstered Colt Peacemaker, a long, wide, curved knife of Oriental aspect swung in a metal-tipped black leather sheath at the left of his gun belt. Directing his attention to the knife, which had a length and heft that beat even the fabled James Black bowie, Smith saw two smaller knives fitted into the sheath behind its fancy, quillonless hilt.

No matter how Poona Woodstole dressed, to Smith he looked like a fine example of British upper class, and the Texan had reason to feel gratitude to one of them. Woodstole was the type of man whose courage, initiative, self-sacrifice and ability had built a tiny

* How this came about is told in *Goodnight's Dream* and *From Hide and Horn*.

island into what, in the 1880's, was the most powerful and respected nation in the world.

"It's here, Wil," Woodstole announced, taking a telegraph form
from his vest pocket. "Cousin Basil's bringing them—"

"Howdy, young feller," Hopkirk boomed, directing his words at
Smith. "Don't recollect seeing you around."

Despite the welcome, Smith guessed that the words had been
uttered as a warning and to direct Woodstole's attention to the fact
that there was a stranger in the office.

"This's Mr. Waxahachie Smith, Poona, Charlie," Wil introduced. "Mr. Smith, meet the owners of the C Lazy P ranch. Charlie Hopkirk and Poona Woodstole."

"Do we say 'Mister' or 'Waxahachie'?" Woodstole inquired
cheerfully, transferring the paper so that he could extend his right
hand.

"Try 'Wax,'" Smith offered, trying to read any hint of guilty
knowledge on the other's face and failing. The hand which closed
on his had strength, without deliberately trying to impress him by
that quality.

"I mind ye pappy when he was running the law in Houston,"
Hopkirk stated, clearly satisfied with the Texan's *bona fides*.
"Wasn't you going to tell Wil something, Poona?"

"I wondered if I'd ever get the chance," Woodstole replied with
a smile.

"Blasted young whippersnapper!" Hopkirk sniffed. "And don't
ask me what one of 'em is, Wax. He taught me to say it. Blasted
Britisher."

"Ignoring the ribald peasantry, Wil," Woodstole began.

"I ain't bald!" the old-timer protested.

Raising his eyes to the roof in a resigned manner, Woodstole
continued, "Cousin Basil is bringing them. He'll be at Laramie on
Friday."

"At Laramie?" Wil repeated. "I don't understand."

"Just one of Basil's precautions," Woodstole explained. "He's
not let us know when he's coming until the last moment. We'll
meet him at Laramie and bring him the rest of the way."

"Both of you?" Wil asked.

"Just me," Hopkirk corrected.

"I believe that Cousin Basil's strong enough to stomach the sight," Woodstole informed the girl. "So Charlie's going. Of course, I'm sending four of the boys along to lessen the blow."

"You're probably wondering what all this is about," Wil remarked to Smith.

"Yes'm."

"Poona's cousin, Sir Basil Houghton-Rand, is British Ambassador in Washington. He's bringing his family jewels, worth five hundred thousand dollars, for us to put on display at the fair."

"That's something I hadn't heard about," Smith said quietly.

"We haven't been spreading it around," Wil admitted. "It's to be in the newspapers around the Territory on Saturday and will be mentioned on the posters I'll have passed around the town over the weekend."

"Five hundred thousand dollars!" Smith exclaimed. "That's a whole slew of money to have on display."

"Pinkertons are guarding it," Woodstole put in. "We're only sending the extra men to cover the last part of the journey so that I can get this old goat out from underfoot for a few days."

"Ranch'll be in ruins and belly-deep in nesters time I get back," Hopkirk declared in a mournful voice. "Still, I've told him so."

"Yes," Wil said to Smith. "They go on like this all the time."

"Sounds that way," the Texan grinned, having caught the undercurrents of mutual respect and affection in the caustic comments and abuse.

Smith had also noticed the change which had come over Wil Jeffreys since the arrival of Woodstole. Gone was much of the businesslike severity and efficiency. Although she seemed to be trying to avoid it, she showed something of the vibrant beautiful woman that lurked beneath her cold exterior. Almost as if reading the Texan's thoughts, Wil picked up her spectacles and brought herself back to the level on which he had first made her acquaintance.

"I've arranged for Mr. Bilak—" she said in an impersonal tone.

"Blasted nester!" spat Hopkirk.

"To come and talk with us," Wil continued as if the interruption had never been made. "He will be meeting us at the mayor's office at noon. I hope that you remembered to bring documentary proof of your title to the C Lazy P land, Poona?"

"I did," the Englishman assured her, tapping a slight bulge on the left side of his vest. "I fetched the deeds with me."

"You've no objection to Mr. Smith being present at the meeting?"

"None, Wil," Woodstole confirmed. "How about Bilak, will he be alone?"

"No," Wil admitted. "He sent word last night that he's bringing one of the Grange's organizers from Cheyenne."

"There ain't but one way to deal with that blasted Grange crowd!" Hopkirk announced, slamming on his Stetson to emphasize his statement. "And it ain't to go sitting guzzling Limey tea 'n' soft-talking all loving with 'em."

"Bloodthirsty old devil, isn't he?" Woodstole sighed, with a languid, disdainful glance at his bristling partner. "Thinks all the world's problems can be solved with war whoops, shooting and scalping."

"You can't talk peaceable to the son of a bit—Grange!" Hopkirk warned, hurriedly revising his final words. "All they want's to grab off land somebody else's come in, tamed and's proved worth having."

Listening to the old-timer, Smith could scent trouble. Maybe Wil Jeffreys had tried to import five known gunfighters to handle the law so that she could compel peace between the ranchers and the homesteaders during the fair. If Woodstole and Hopkirk had learned of his coming, they might have sent Hardy's party to stop him. Except that neither had given any hint that they might object to his presence. Nor did they appear to have taken any action against Ottaway.

"I think you'd best head for Laramie *before* the meeting," Woodstole declared to the old-timer. "Don't mind him, Wax. He always gets this way if I let him go out in the rain. It must rust what passes for his brains."

"Just for that," Hopkirk threatened, "I've a danged good mind to go *afore* it and leave you to handle them ba—Grange *gentlemen* yourself."

"Come on. If you'll promise to go, I'll buy you a stirrup cup to speed you on your way," Woodstole answered. "We'll see you at noon, Wil."

"That will give me time to show Mr. Smith the marshal's office," Wil replied. "Unless you have other plans, Mr. Smith?"

"Nary a plan, ma'am," Smith admitted, drawing on his glove and taking his hat from where it swung by its chin strap on the back of his chair. "It'll help if you're along to talk to your marshal."

The three men accompanied Wil from her office. Informing her tellers that she would not be back until one o'clock, she led the way to the front door. Following close behind, Smith heard Wil's sharp intake of breath and saw her pause with her hand on the handle. He looked over her shoulder and through the door's glass panel, wanting to find out what had caused the reaction. Carrying a canvas bag and dressed as she had been in the barroom the previous night, Lily Shivers was strolling across the street. Stiffening her shoulders, as if going to face an unpleasant ordeal, Wil opened the door and stepped out onto the sidewalk.

"Hi, Poona, Charlie," Lily greeted as the men emerged from the bank, then indicated a pair of excellent saddle horses standing tied to its hitching rail. "I thought I knew those two flea-bitten, cow-hocked crowbait when I saw them. Well, hello there, Wax." She looked at the badge on his vest for a moment. "I didn't know I was entertaining the town's new marshal last night."

"Neither did I," Smith admitted.

"Sure hope it won't stop you coming with Poona and Charlie to the party on Saturday night," Lily went on.

"Party?" Hopkirk put in, displaying lively interest. "What party?"

"It's what you might call my un-wedding party," Lily explained, and held up a left hand devoid of rings. "My divorce's come through at last, boys, and I'm a free woman again."

"Do you want to see me, Miss Shiver?" Wil asked, with icicles in her voice.

"At the party?" the blonde grinned. "Why it'd be a pleasure and a sure-enough delight to have my banker and the town's esteemed mayor as a guest."

"I mean now!" Wil gritted, knowing that several "good" women were watching and being aware of how they felt about the owner of the Happy Bull saloon.

"Nope," Lily answered, sharing Wil's knowledge without it causing her any concern. "I was just going to pay some money into the bank. Old Ryall likes me to come dressed this ways, it gives him pleasure to see a real woman in there." She had raised her voice, to make sure the listening women could hear. When Wil did not speak, she went on louder than was necessary, "Say, though, why don't all of you come on over, have a snifter on the house and take a look at the new sign I'm having painted special in honor of the county fair?"

"It might prove interesting," Wil replied, contriving to sound as if she doubted that it would. "Unfortunately, we all have other things to attend to."

"That's our mayor talking," Lily said, in mock admiration. "Always business first with him—her. Why Wil's a regular day-and-night, rip-roaring business*man.* Isn't she, Poona?"

Stiffening slightly and losing his smile, Woodstole made no reply. A red flush crept into Wil's cheeks, but she said nothing.

Watching the byplay, Smith could almost smell the waves of hostility flowing between the two women. They could be caused from jealousy over a mutual interest in the British rancher. Or they might have older, deeper roots. Either way, Smith's work could be adversely affected. As far as he had seen last night, Lily ran a clean, well-kept, honest place. Unless he missed his guess, it would be the gathering point for the male civic dignitaries and important visitors. In consequence, it would need supervision to prevent any untoward incidents occurring. Lily's wholehearted cooperation would be needed in that.

Which posed a question.

Would Lily Shivers' obvious hatred of Wil Jeffreys cause her to try to spoil the fair and discredit the town?

If so, Lily could have learned of Wil sending for Smith and the other gunfighters. She had been in Laramie when Smith arrived and might have sent for Hardy to meet them at Gilpin's way station to prevent him reaching Widow's Creek. Her mention of having seen the gambler coming from Wil's private office could have been said to make him distrust his employer. There were a number of explanations why Poona Woodstole's name had been imprinted on the paper found by Capey, all innocent, if Lily had sent it.

"Come on, Charlie, Poona," Lily continued after a moment. "You can make time to see it. And I'll bet Wil's just itching to take a look. Only she's one business*man* who doesn't dare come into a saloon."

"I'm not particularly interested—" Wil gritted.

"Maybe we'd best take a look at it, Miss Jeffreys," Smith suggested, recalling the blonde's comments the previous night and deciding that the new sign might be worth seeing before its completion and erection. "It'll not take us far out of our way, or much of our time."

"And you'll have a snort of Old Stump-Blaster before you look?" Lily inquired, flickering a long, appraising look at Smith.

"Not right now, ma'am," the Texan refused.

"No drinking on duty, huh, Wax?" the blonde challenged.

"It's a right good rule to stay alive by," Smith answered. "But I'll hold you to the offer when I'm not."

"Maybe it won't be open then," Lily warned.

Smith looked at the blonde, meeting her eyes until she turned her head. Up to the conversation, he had liked Lily and respected her as a shrewd woman competing in a man's world on male terms. By her behavior, she was asking to forfeit his friendship and respect.

"I've bought my own liquor afore and expect to again," Smith told her.

"So you finally got free from that no-account varmint, Lily," Hopkirk put in, clearly considering that the subject should be changed. His diplomacy did not continue. "He wasn't never a lick of good. Wil had the right notion when she told him to go to hell."

"Wil's always been the one for right notions," Lily replied, and the edge of bitterness in her voice gave Smith an inkling of the cause of the girl's enmity. Then she gave a harsh, mirthless laugh. "Come and see the sign. It's in the back room, but maybe our mayor daren't go through the front door into a saloon—?"

"There's a door around ba—" Hopkirk began.

"I don't suppose I'll get too contaminated, the short time I'll be inside," Wil interrupted, stepping by Lily as if the blonde did not exist and starting to cross the street. "It can't be as bad as all that."

If looks could have killed, Wil would not have taken three steps before she died. Lily showed all the symptoms of a gambler whose bluff had been called. Clenching her fists and gritting her teeth, Lily led the men after the other girl. Going by the few horses secured to the saloon's hitching rail, Wil stepped up and crossed the sidewalk with an air of cold determination. Even so, she seemed to hesitate at the batwing doors. Then she pushed them open and stepped through.

Trailing along behind the girls, Smith glanced at the horses. Two had army McClellan saddles and stood a few feet away from three which toted Texas rigs. The latter had no special significance, for many Texans rode the Wyoming ranges. At that moment, Smith was more interested in watching Lily and Wil.

Already the saloon was doing a brisk trade. The arrival of the mayor caused surprise, if not actual consternation, among the majority of people in the barroom. Townsmen stopped their conversations, put down their drinks and stared at Wil. A low giggle broke from one of Lily's girls, but the remainder scowled their animosity at the invasion of their domain by a "good" woman—and one who their well-liked boss had reason to hate.

Always alert, as a man in his line of work must be to remain alive, Smith scanned the room for enemies. His attention came to rest on three men standing at the bar. All had their backs to him and two of them held their heads inclined forward so that he could see no more than the tops of their hats reflected in the big mirror behind the bar. Tall, wearing ordinary cowhand clothing in the fashion of the Southern ranges, gun-hung, they might have been no more than a trio of ranch employees visiting the town's best saloon to see how it stacked up in comparison with their more usual haunts north of the river.

Glancing at the newcomers reflected in the mirror, the man whose face Smith could see—but did not recognize—addressed his companions. Up tilted the Stetsons, while hands crept surreptitiously toward the butts of guns. Two tanned, unshaven, heavily mustached faces came into view. Smith identified them as belonging to the Sheppey brothers, Arnie and Tod. What was more, Smith could guess how they would react to being in the same room as himself.

"Look out!" Smith barked.

Giving the warning, he lunged to the right and away from the rest of his party. Flying across as he moved, his left fingers met and closed on the right glove. There would be little enough time for him to save his life. Already the three men were turning from the bar and drawing their revolvers.

At Smith's words and the sight of the trio of customers' behavior, Lily dived to the left and down. Showing an equally astute and rapid grasp of the situation, Wil matched her blond rival's movements. They landed side by side on the floor, flattening belly-down regardless of the layer of sawdust that covered it, and stayed there.

Continuing the motion which snatched his right hand from its leather covering, Smith snapped out, cocked and fired the slip gun in a single blur of motion. At the end of his sideways bound, he let both legs bend until he was crouching almost on his knees and with a considerable decrease in his normal height. Lead from Arnie Sheppey's Colt passed about Smith's head, but he had assumed the stooping posture in time to save himself from injury.

By the time Smith's bullets reached Tod Sheppey, always the faster of the brothers, they had separated a little from their line-ahead flight. Three holes formed a small triangle in Tod's forehead just before his brother got off a shot. Jerking, Tod staggered against the third man and disturbed his aim. Although Tod's Colt cracked, it had been fired by a dead hand and its bullet did no more than spike a hole in the floorboards at the far side of the room.

Although concentrating on the three men at the bar, Smith was also aware of how his companions were reacting. Reflected in the mirror, he saw the women sensibly throwing themselves out of the danger area. Woodstole and Hopkirk clearly intended to take a more aggressive role in the proceedings.

Which could prove mighty dangerous for Smith, if it had been the Englishman who sent the three killers to meet him at Gilpin's way station.

Flashing across at some speed, Woodstole's right hand gripped and slid the big knife from its fancy black sheath. It had a blade as strange and Oriental-looking as its hilt. Extending straight from the bolster of the hilt for about six inches, the back of the blade curved downward to form the upper curve of the spearpoint.* At first narrow, the blade's cutting edge widened into a semicircle to complete the point. An inch ahead of the choil on the edge, a notch like a very shallow "W" had been cut.

To eyes accustomed to American knives, the weapon drawn by the Englishman appeared heavy, awkward and badly balanced. Certainly it did not seem to be the kind of knife a man would select if he intended to attack an enemy standing several yards away, the distance separating Smith's party from the trio at the bar.

Carrying the knife around and out to the extent of his right arm, Woodstole pivoted on his left foot and carried the right forward to stride in Smith's direction.

* A knife is described with the cutting edge downward, the hilt to the viewer's left and point to his right.

9

The Happy Bull's New Sign

Even as Woodstole's actions sent a warning screaming through Smith, while the slip gun's barrel pointed up from the recoil, the Englishman continued his movements. About to throw himself sideways and, if he avoided the attack, turn his Colt on his assailant, Smith saw Woodstole swing away from him.

Swirling around on his right foot, the Englishman whipped the knife forward parallel to the ground. Giving a sharp, snapping motion to his wrist, he flung his weapon in Arnie Sheppey's direction. Doing so caused it to spin around on a slightly upward plane and pass through the air with an audible "whoosh!" Luck, or an accurate estimation of distance and the revolutions of the knife, caused the blade to be swinging inward as it reached the man.

Razor-sharp steel sliced into Sheppey's Adam's apple, the weight of the knife and its spinning flight's momentum driving it deeper and deeper. Dropping the smoking, uncocked revolver, he clawed unavailingly at the strangely shaped weapon which protruded from his throat. With his life's blood spurting from the wound, he tottered around in a crazy circle and collapsed.

Struck by Tod's staggering body as he cut loose, the third man knew that he had missed Smith. Although he was aware that Woodstole had selected the other brother as target for the strange knife, the man knew that he still was not out of danger. Dragging out his old Army Colt, Hopkirk slanted its eight-inch-long barrel in the man's direction.

With commendable speed, the man's left hand caught hold of Tod's sleeve. A surging heave sent the stricken Tod reeling to intercept the bullet fired by the old rancher. Having protected himself, the man flung himself across the room. Gun in hand, he sped along parallel to the counter. Both of the bartenders ducked out of sight. Women screamed and men hurled themselves to the floor, or crouched behind tables. In doing so, they effectively prevented Smith and Hopkirk from taking shots at the departing man. Ducking his head down and left shoulder forward, he plunged through a side window to disappear from view.

Regaining an upright position, Smith leapt in pursuit. Charging through the excited occupants of the room, he flattened himself against the wall by the window. Fast as he had moved, on peering cautiously out he found that the man had acted even faster. On quitting the building, he must have landed running for he was nowhere to be seen.

Smith remembered the horses at the hitching rail. Three carried double-girthed saddles such as Texans, many New Mexicans of Anglo-Saxon origin and Arizonans used. The Sheppey brothers hailed from the latter Territory. Deciding that the horses belonged to the trio, he sprinted toward the batwing doors. Already Hopkirk and Woodstole, the latter now holding an Artillery Model Peacemaker, were preparing to go out through them. Joining them, Smith plunged onto the sidewalk. He landed ready to throw lead. There was no need. The man had not come around the front to collect the means of making good his mistake.

"Blast it!" Hopkirk spat out. "He's hornswoggled us."

"Round the back!" Woodstole went on.

Although the three men ran to the corner, through the alley and to the rear of the building, they saw no sign of the third man. He had clearly wasted no time in leaving the vicinity of the saloon. Nor did there appear to be anybody around who could shed light on the direction he had taken.

"We've lost him!" Hopkirk declared, angrily thrusting the Army Colt back into its holster.

"If it's not a personal question," Woodstole remarked to Smith as they returned their weapons to leather and retracted their footsteps along the alley, "who were those chaps?"

"I don't know the feller who got away," Smith admitted. "But the other two're Tod 'n' Arnie Sheppey. I shot their brother down in Arizona a couple of years back. Word's been going 'round that they was gunning for me on 'count of it."

"Come up here a-hunting for you, huh?" suggested Hopkirk.

"More likely they just happened to be around," Smith answered. "Knew I'd recognize them and started to stop me doing it out loud. There's a bounty on each of their scalps." Then he recalled something. "I haven't thanked you two gents for siding me in there."

"Had to do something, old boy," Woodstole drawled, in a languid manner which did not match the speed he had shown in drawing and throwing the knife. "Those blighters looked a bit aggressive and had to be stopped before somebody was hurt."

"Didn't reckon you could take the three of 'em, neither," Hopkirk continued. "So I cut loose with my old Colt 'n' Poona started tossing his *kukri* around. Danged heathen weapon."

"Your *what*?" Smith asked the Englishman.

"*Kukri,*" Woodstole elaborated. "I learned how to use it while I was serving with the Gurkhas in Poona."

"They're some blasted Injun tribe in what he says's the real Injia," Hopkirk explained. "Like I tell him, our Injun's allus been real enough for me."

Smith knew that Great Britain ruled a country called India. There was more than a hint of military training about Woodstole. According to what he had said, some of his service had been with the native troops who used the strange kind of knife he carried. That reference to Poona accounted for his unusual first name. Maybe, like Smith, he had been christened after the town of his birth.

However, at that moment Smith felt less interested in the Englishman's past than about the present. If Woodstole and Hopkirk had wanted him dead, they could have achieved their ends by not moving so fast, letting the Sheppey boys kill him and then wiping them out. That last would have prevented the brothers from answering questions in the event of their capture. Smith was inclined to believe that finding Woodstole's name on the message had been no more than a coincidence. He must look elsewhere for the person who wanted to have him gunned down.

Did the answer await him inside the saloon?

Going in ahead of the ranchers, Smith found Wil and Lily on their feet. Brushing the sawdust from her dress, Lily was telling the customers to go ahead with whatever they had been doing before the fuss. Although slightly paler than when she had entered, Wil looked composed and tidied her appearance with steady hands. Both girls turned toward the men.

"He got away," Lily remarked, stating the obvious.

"Clean away," Smith agreed, and searched her face for any sign of relief at the news. "How long had they been in here?"

"Since just after we opened," Lily replied, showing no emotion and meeting his gaze without wavering. "You knew them?"

"Only the two who took lead," Smith answered. "Have they been in here afore?"

"Not that I could swear to. But I don't recall every feller's comes. I'll ask around among the boys and girls for you."

"I'd be right obliged if you would," Smith drawled.

Armed with shotguns, the town marshal and two deputies arrived. Tall, burly Marshal Caster was a different class of peace officer than Sheriff McCobb and looked poorly dressed enough to be honest. He did not impress Smith as being an office-filler. Studying him, Smith wondered why he had agreed to stand down during the fair. It might have been an opportunity for him to impress important visitors and maybe gain employment in a larger town.

Showing some surprise at finding the mayor in the saloon, Caster did not allow it to distract him. He asked what had been the cause of the trouble and listened while Woodstole, Hopkirk and Smith told their stories. All the time, his eyes roamed over Smith.

"Seems like they was hunting you, Mr. Smith," Caster commented at last.

"Looks that way," Smith admitted noncommittally, watching Lily to see how she took his remark on the trio's motives. Nothing showed and he went on, "The Sheppey boys're wanted down to Prescott. There's seven hundred and fifty dollars on each of 'em."

"And you aim to claim it?" Caster said coldly.

"That's what rewards are put on for, marshal," Smith replied.

"Can't say I've ever took much to bounty hunters," Caster stated.

"And I don't take to local peace officers who pull out when the going looks like it's getting tough," Smith answered.

Remembering what Wil had told him during the opening stages of their interview, Smith realized that he was doing Caster an injustice. Always a believer in fair play, the Texan was prepared to forget his annoyance at the marshal's comment about bounty hunters.

"That was my decision rather than Marshal Caster's," Wil put in. "It took some argument before he agreed. The marshal's got a lot of friends in and around town and they'll all be here for the fair—"

"So he doesn't want to rile 'em by arresting them or *their* friends, which he might have to do, while they're celebrating," Smith drawled. "That's smart thinking seeing's how he'll be handling the new law here long after we're gone."

"Yes, Mr. Smith," Wil said with a smile. "You're hired as whipping boys, if you know what I mean."

"I've heard tell about them," Smith declared. "And, for what you're paying me, folks can whip ahead."

Caster had continued to study the Texan. In his time as a peace officer, the marshal had been brought into contact with a number of professional bounty hunters. He knew that the majority of them were cold-blooded killers little better morally than the wanted men they hunted down. While Ottaway, whom he had already met, struck Caster as being close to that kind, he sensed that Smith was different. His every instinct, combined with some knowledge of Smith's past, told him that the Texan would be hard but fair in the execution of the difficult work ahead. More than that, Smith accepted how he had been brought in to face the objections of citizens who ran foul of the law during the celebrations at the fair. When it was over, those same citizens would have no cause to hold grudges against their regular law enforcement officers.

"I shouldn't have said what I did about bounty hunters, Mr. Smith," Caster apologized.

"Why not, if you feel that way on it?" Smith answered. "I don't

go much for 'em myself. But if I have to down somebody with a
bounty on his head, I'll claim it. If I don't, somebody with no right
to the money will."

"Likely," the marshal conceded. "Do you want to take over
today?"

"If that'll be all right with you," the Texan replied. "There's no
rush, one way or the other."

"If it suits you, I'll show you 'round the town afore I start my
vacation," Caster offered.

"I'd be right obliged if you would," Smith agreed, knowing it
would be folly to refuse such valuable information.

"Let me tend to things here," Caster suggested. "Then we can
get to it."

"I've got to go to a meeting with Miss Jeffreys at noon," Smith
drawled. "Shouldn't last more than an hour—"

"Not that long, if I've my way," Hopkirk growled.

"If it's all right with you," Smith continued to the marshal,
"we'll meet up, take a meal at the Simple Hotel and talk some."

"That's all right with me," Caster agreed. "Go through their
pockets, boys, then have them toted to the undertaker's."

"Sure, Bert," answered the older of the deputies.

"Want to see what they're carrying, friend?" the marshal inquired.

"Don't reckon it'll be anything to interest me," Smith replied,
determined to keep Lily—if she should be involved—convinced
that he suspected nothing. "And you can say 'Wax,' if it comes
easier than 'friend.'"

"Hey, Wax," Lily remarked as the marshal and his deputies
went to attend to their work. "How about coming to see the new
sign?"

"Why not," the Texan replied. "That's what we're here for."

While the others had been talking, Woodstole had collected the
kukri and borrowed a rag from behind the bar to wipe off the
blood. Slipping the curved blade back into its sheath, he followed
the others to the back room. Throwing open its door with a flourish, Lily waved for them to precede her. Inside the room, a slim

young man wearing a paint-spattered smock stopped his work on the long board set up against the far wall.

"Well?" Lily asked, with a challenging, defiant grin.

Although not yet completed, the picture on the board had sufficient detail for Wil, Smith and the ranchers to know what it would depict. A very obvious bull stood proudly in the center of a group of equally obvious cows. Every external anatomical feature had been marked in prominently.

"Good God!" Wil gasped. "You can't mean to put that thing up?"

"Why not?" the blonde demanded. "That sure is one happy bull, don't you reckon, Poona?"

"Possibly," the Englishman answered, and his voice had lost all its earlier cordiality.

"I can't allow it to be put up!" Wil stated.

"*You* can't?" Lily challenged.

"As mayor of Widow's Creek, I have a responsibility to the town—"

"Just how do you reckon to stop me putting it up?" the blonde interrupted.

"Any way I have to," Wil warned.

"Such as?" Lily demanded.

There was a savage, brittle air of tension in the room. The two beautiful women were eyeing each other like alley cats meeting on a fence top. If Wil had been another saloon-worker, Smith would have expected claws to be raking at flesh. As it was, the lady banker stood with clenched fists and bust heaving. Facing her, Lily crooked long-nailed fingers and seemed to be crouching ready to meet any kind of attack her enemy chose to launch.

"We've that meeting soon, Wil," Woodstole remarked quietly. "It wouldn't do for us to keep Mr. Bilak waiting."

The soft-spoken words sounded loud and broke the tension. Letting out her held-back breath in a long sigh, Wil opened her hands.

"You're right, Poona," she said, hardly louder than a whisper. "Shall we go, gentlemen?"

"How about my new sign?" Lily insisted. "What do you think of it, Poona?"

"We'll go, Wil," the Englishman said, and turned on his heel.

Lily stared at the departing ranchers with more than a hint of consternation, as if realizing that she had gone too far. Watching her, Smith could see the worry on her face and thought that she might relent. Instead, she braced back her shoulders and tightened her lips in lines of grim determination.

"Don't put it up, Shivers!" Wil snapped, swinging away from the blonde and leaving the room.

"Don't hell!" Lily hissed and lunged forward with fingers curved like talons ready to drive into flesh.

"Hold it!" Smith snapped, shooting out his left hand to catch the blonde by her right bicep and bringing her to a halt.

"Take your hand off me!" Lily spat.

"Not until you show sense," the Texan replied, and glared at the painter. "If you want to stay healthy, stand right where you are."

Although he had been tensing as if to leap to the blonde's rescue, the artist refrained from doing so. He could see the anger of Smith's face and read it in the Texan's voice. That was the man who had killed another human being across the width of the bar-room and in an incredibly swift movement. There had been no hesitation in how Smith had acted then and the man sensed there would be none if he disobeyed the grim command.

"I thought we were friends, Smith!" Lily said bitterly, standing still.

"So did I," the Texan answered. "Same's I thought you were a smart woman up until we come in here." He released his hold. "Do you reckon even your friends'd stand for you jumping her over that blasted sign? They'd have you closed up afore sundown."

"You'd close me down," Lily corrected.

"If I was told and figured I'd good cause," Smith agreed. "Which I reckon I'd have if you put it up."

"I hate Wil Jeffreys' guts!"

"That figures. And she doesn't cotton none to you either, I'd say. Only this's not just between you and her anymore, Lily. Put up that sign and you'll be rubbing the whole town's face in the dirt."

"It's a chance I'm game to take!"

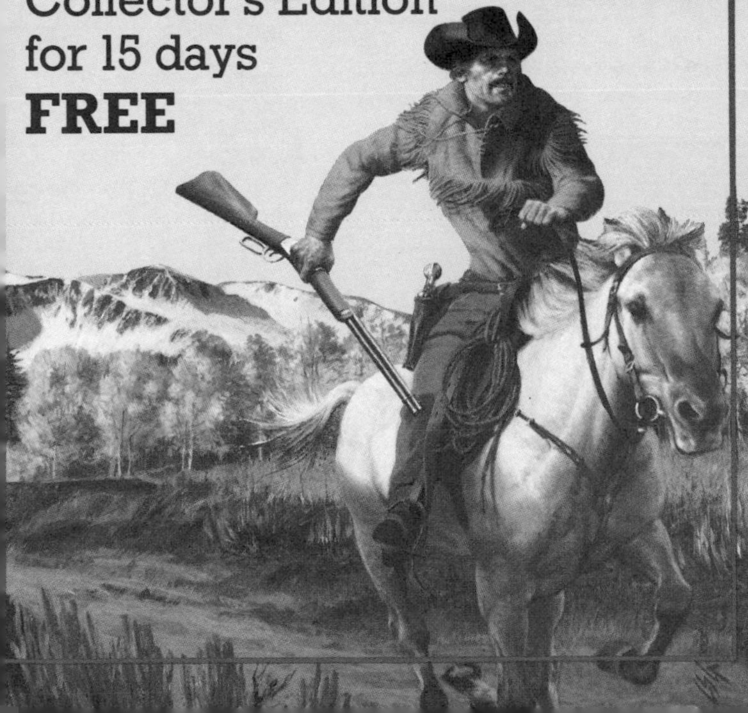

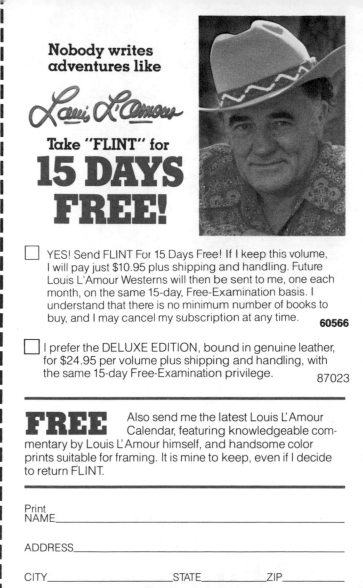

BUSINESS REPLY MAIL
FIRST CLASS   PERMIT NO. 2154   HICKSVILLE, N.Y.

Postage will be paid by addressee:

The Louis L'Amour Collection

Bantam Books
P.O. Box 956
Hicksville, New York 11802-9829

NO POSTAGE
NECESSARY
IF MAILED
IN THE
UNITED STATES

"Then you've not got the good sense you'd made me figure you for having."

"I'm putting that sign up, Wax!" Lily declared grimly. "And there's only one person who can stop me."

"Who'd that be?" the Texan asked.

"Wil Jeffreys," Lily replied, glancing at the open door. "You tell her from me that she'll have to come and beg me not to put it up."

10

A Man of Direct Action

On leaving the back room, Smith found Wil and the marshal standing close to the open door. Apparently Caster had just joined the mayor, but Wil's face showed that she had overheard the conversation—particularly Lily's conditions for not putting up the sign. However, Wil made no mention of it, but stood stiffly, almost at attention, with tight lips and angry eyes, as Caster addressed the Texan.

"They'd about sixty dollars apiece on them, Wax. Nothing else."

"Their maw and pappy run a cap-and-ball outfit down near Tucson," Smith replied. "Pima County sheriff'll know it and can take Tod 'n' Arnie's leavings to them. Their horses and gear'll sell for something and, likely, their folks could use the money. Did you look in their saddles?"

"I will, when I find them," Caster promised.

"Aren't they at the hitching rail?"

"Nope. Them three belong to the Rocking V boys over by the chuck-a-luck table."

"Are they local hands?" Smith inquired, glancing at the men indicated by the marshal.

"Come from over on the Antelopes," Caster answered. "Not what you'd call next-door neighbors."

Not, Smith admitted to himself, that the proximity of the trio's ranch would prove anything. It was unlikely that Woodstole and Hopkirk could identify every horse in their immediate neighbors' *remudas*, especially when the animals had been standing with their right, unbranded, sides showing as the ranchers walked by. The three cowhands wore Texas-style clothing and so were almost certain to use double-girthed rigs. So Hopkirk and his partner had duplicated Smith's mistake in the matter of who owned the horses.

"The meeting, Mr. Smith!" Wil prompted, glancing at the door of the back room in a pointed manner.

Suddenly the Texan realized that the black-haired beauty was straining every nerve and fiber to hold her temper in control. Wil had the expression of a woman who had all but reached the end of her tether. Thinking back to comments made the previous night, he decided that the new sign was only the latest of a series of actions by Lily aimed at goading and humiliating Wil. If the blonde should come out of the room, Wil might not be able to restrain her anger. Then there would be an unpleasant, ugly scene, if nothing worse.

"Sure, Miss Jeffreys," Smith drawled. "We'd best get to it. I'll see you at one, Bert."

"That'll give me time to go around and pick up those jaspers' horses, if I can find them," Caster replied. "Their sidekick'll be long gone by now, I'd say."

"It's not likely he'd hang around," Smith agreed. "I'll see you, then."

While crossing to the batwing doors, Smith hoped that he would be able to discover the cause of the hatred existing between Wil and Lily. If he knew that, he could estimate how much danger or difficulty it posed to him in his work as temporary marshal. There was no direct evidence to connect the blonde with Hardy, or the Sheppey brothers. Even the latter being in the saloon without horses close by could have an innocent explanation. Smith decided that he must have a long and confidential talk with his employer before sundown. Until then, he would walk warily—especially in Lily's presence.

The ranchers were waiting on the sidewalk when Wil and Smith emerged from the saloon. That ended his hopes of satisfying his curiosity straightaway. None of them spoke as they walked away from the Happy Bull and Smith reconciled himself to waiting for a more opportune moment to talk privately with the mayor.

The silence continued as they entered a large square with a neatly laid-out garden in its center. On each side of the square stood civic buildings, or the homes of prominent citizens. Smith guessed that this was the center of the town, socially and administratively if not geographically.

Several farmers hovered in front of the big, stone-built town hall, which also housed the court and law enforcement offices, on the western side of the square. Among the crowd, two men caught Smith's eye. Tall, slim, in their early twenties, they dressed like their companions, but their sallow, hollow-cheeked faces did not indicate long hours spent working in the open. Smoking what looked like hand-rolled cigarettes, they kept their gaze on Wil's party and twisted their loose lips in mocking sneers.

Followed by the farmer who had traveled on the stagecoach with Smith, a big bearded man left the crowd.

"Good morning, Mr. Bilak," Wil greeted.

"Miss Jeffreys," the big man replied, without a trace of an accent. "This's Cyrus Cushman. I said he would be coming to the meeting."

"I'm pleased to meet you, Mr. Cushman," Wil stated, shaking hands. "Shall we go inside, gentlemen?"

"See you brought friends along, Bilak," Hopkirk growled as they entered the building.

"The Patrons of Husbandry is a democratic organization," Cushman answered, instead of the Grange's local representative. "Its members are permitted to attend any meeting which may concern them."

"Was it your idea to have them come along?" Smith inquired as he, the ranchers and the Grange's representatives followed Wil into the building.

"They came of their own free will," Cushman declared, eyeing the Texan with open distrust and thinly veiled hostility. "But I don't understand your presence."

"I asked Mr. Smith to come," Wil told the man. "He is town marshal as of today and I felt that his presence was necessary. Do *you* object, Mr. Bilak?"

"Can't say I do, Wil," the burly man replied.

"I thought this blasted meeting was supposed to be secret,"

Hopkirk challenged. "We didn't bring in any of our boys on account that it was."

Again Smith felt uneasy stirrings inside him. If the meeting was supposed to be held in secret, somebody had betrayed it to the homesteaders. That same person might be hoping to ruin any hope of peace between the ranchers and the nesters. Did this desire tie in with the attempts on Smith's life? Whoever had learned about the meeting could also have gained information concerning his coming and taken steps to stop him arriving.

Smith studied Bilak as the party entered a big room on the ground floor. There was nothing of the newly arrived immigrant about the burly farmer. If his lack of accent and appearance were anything to go by, he had been many years in the United States and might even have been born there. Such a man would be aware of Smith's potential in the event of a range war and might suspect that the Texan's sympathies could rest with the cattle industry.

The Grange, the Patrons of Husbandry, was a very vocal organization devoted to protecting the interests of farmers. Nor did it restrict itself to words. On occasion, the Grange was said to have resorted to more violent means when talking had failed to bring about the desired results. If they had decided on direct action against the C Lazy P, the local chapter of the Grange could have concluded that Smith's presence in Widow's Creek would be detrimental to their plans. Maybe Bilak had been behind Hardy, Moxley and Hayward. He could even have marked his message with Poona Woodstole's name in case the affair went the wrong way, to throw suspicion onto his enemy.

"I'll stand, if you don't mind, ma'am," Smith drawled as Wil waved the men to take seats around the long table in the center of the room.

Leaning his right shoulder against the wall, close to the handle side of the door through which they had entered, Smith watched Wil take her place at the head of the table. Going around, the two farmers sat on her left and the ranchers faced them. For all her experiences at the Happy Bull, Wil seemed perfectly composed and her usual efficient self as she got down to business.

"Well, gentlemen," she said. "I asked you to meet here, on neutral ground, so that you can clarify the situation regarding the land north of the Elk Fork. Mr. Woodstole has brought the deeds to his property for your inspection."

"Here they are," the Englishman drawled, drawing a long, bulky envelope from inside his shirt. "My partner and I'll be pleased to answer any points you raise."

"These give you title to twenty miles of land between the Widow's and Owl Creeks of the Elk Fork," Cushman said grudgingly after examining the documents. "That's a lot of land for two men to own."

"It was offered for homesteading six years back," Hopkirk pointed out. "Only there weren't any takers. So the land office at Cheyenne sold it to Poona and me. And I'll be—"

"If you'd seen the land when we first came, you'd have known why it wasn't homesteaded," Woodstole interrupted, silencing his old partner with a warning glare. "I think you can remember it, Mr. Bilak."

"I can," Bilak confirmed. "And I was one of the men who refused the offer to homestead it. These papers are proof enough for me—"

"How about the Jones family, Mr. Woodstole?" Cushman demanded. "They complained to my chapter of the Grange that you ran them off their land *south* of the Elk Fork."

"Did we?" challenged the Englishman. "Perhaps Mr. Bilak can explain things?"

"They'd been taking C Lazy P cattle," Bilak stated. "That's why I refused to back them up."

"Understand this, Mr. Cushman," Woodstole went on. "Charlie and I have never stopped farmers hunting deer or elk on our range. Nor would we begrudge hungry families the odd steer for their own table. But the Joneses didn't let it stop there. Marshal Caster found evidence that they were butchering our cattle and selling the meat and hides."

"And we didn't run 'em off," Hopkirk announced. "Afore we could do that, they'd hightailed it out of this neck of the woods."

"That was after I refused to give them the Grange's protection,"

Bilak elaborated. "Mr. Woodstole and Mr. Hopkirk could've set the law on them, but didn't."

"I knew nothing of this," Cushman declared. "Naturally, when we heard their story and compl— When they told us what had happened, I was sent here to investigate the affairs."

"They complained about me?" Bilak asked.

"Yes," admitted Cushman. "We had to check. You know there's been discontent among our members."

An uneasy silence followed the words and Cushman's face showed that he felt he had said too much. Since the senior officials of the Grange had started to advocate a policy of live-and-let-live where ranching interests were concerned, some of the more radical and militant members had grown restless, or even formed opposition groups of their own. As could only be expected, the offshoots had attracted dangerous fanatics and political opportunists who saw advancement for themselves and their beliefs by giving verbal support to farmers or would-be homesteaders at odds with the Grange.

While one of the saner, more realistic members of the Grange, who had become reconciled with the fact that ranchers and farmers must coexist to survive, Cushman did not wish the affairs of the Patrons of Husbandry discussed before nonmembers. So he looked at Wil in search of a change of subject. It came, but the lady mayor did not supply it.

Following the conversation, Smith became aware of a disturbance in the hall beyond the room. Feet clattered and voices lifted in protest or recrimination. Then the door flew open and the two sallow-featured young men burst in. Some feet behind them, the remainder of the crowd from the square surged by the clerks who had tried to prevent the interruption to the meeting.

"Remember the Jon—!" began the taller of the pair.

Whatever else he had planned to say ended abruptly. At the first hint of trouble, Smith moved from his place against the wall. Pushing himself forward, he pivoted on his right foot and drove the toe of his other boot with considerable force against the speaker's testicles. Startled exclamations from the men at the table mingled with the sound of chairs being thrown over and the stricken intruder's strangled screech of agony. Clutching at the injured region, he buckled at the knees and fell writhing to the floor.

Mouth open to yell, the second young man made no more than a gurgle of surprise as his companion went down. Allowing the first one to blunder helplessly by him, Smith dealt just as swiftly with the second. From snatching off his right glove, the Texan whipped his left fist around and up. Holding his fingers tightly clenched, he crashed the protruding second knuckle in a backhand blow to the center of the sallow face. Back curled Smith's right hand, drawing the slip gun and presenting it, full cocked, at the faces of the nearest farmers. He gave no attention to the second man, who went sprawling facedown in the left side corner.

"I'll kill the next man to set foot in here," Smith stated, with calm and chillingly menacing assurance. "And the same applies to any man I find holding a gun when I turn 'round to the table."

"Hold it, all of you!" roared Ottaway's voice from the front entrance of the town hall. "We've got scatterguns here for them's don't."

While surprised to find Ottaway showing such initiative and sense of duty, Smith wasted no time in thinking about it. Throwing looks at the speaker, the crowd halted their hostile intentions and stood still.

"Mind what I said, at the table!" Smith ordered over his shoulder. "I'm turning 'round now."

On swinging toward the center of the room, Smith saw Hopkirk returning the Army Colt to its holster. None of the others, not even Woodstole, had drawn a weapon. For their part, the two officials of the Grange showed such surprise and annoyance at the interruption that Smith felt sure they had known nothing about it. Satisfied that he had displayed his impartiality, Smith stepped out of the room. Ottaway and young Jeffreys stood at the entrance to the hall, shotguns covering the farmers. An air of alert eagerness transformed the young man's face.

"Heard there was going to be trouble, Wax," Ottaway announced. "So we got the scatters and came to take cards."

"Good thinking," Smith replied. "Mr. Bilak. Come and ask your folks to leave peaceable."

"Who's idea was this?" Bilak demanded, glaring at the crowd as he stepped out of the room.

"Them two young fellers said we should come in and stand up for the Joneses, Zorin," answered a blond-haired man of Teutonic appearance. "Said they'd come to see justice done."

"I told you why the Grange wouldn't support them!" Bilak barked. "Now get over the river and wait at the Busted Plow until I'm through."

"We thought you'd need help," the blonde muttered.

"If I do, I'll ask for it," Bilak replied. "This whole thing was going right and peaceful until you let them come busting in."

Bilak clearly retained control over the other farmers, for there was no argument against his orders. Muttering to themselves, the crowd withdrew from the town hall. As a sign of his good faith, Smith returned the Colt to its holster and went into the meeting room. Carrying the shotguns on the crooks of their left arms, Ottaway and young Jeffreys followed him. Wil stared at her brother, but did not get the opportunity to question him about his presence.

"Who're these two?" Ottaway asked, indicating the prostrate intruders.

"I didn't see them outside," Cushman growled.

"They were in the crowd," Smith pointed out. "Do you know them?"

"That I do. And if I'd seen them, I'd have mentioned it."

"Who are they?" Ottaway insisted.

"Their names are Landers and Wymar, or something like that," Cushman supplied. "I've seen them in Cheyenne with that damned Free Land bunch."

That explained the Grange leader's hostility toward the young men. Most radical of all the groups to split away from the Patrons of Husbandry, the Free Land Society had the worst reputation as troublemakers. Organized by intellectual young graduates of Eastern colleges, it advocated that all land must be free and open to everybody, a policy which did not appeal to wealthy members of the Grange any more than to the ranchers.

An incident like the Jones family's flight to avoid justice, carefully distorted, offered an ideal medium for the Free Land agitators to work on. They knew how to play off antipathy toward the ranchers against greed and avarice and weld all the emotions into achieving their ends.

Naturally observant, Smith had studied the young men outside and concluded that, no matter how they dressed, they were not farmers. He had heard about the activities of Free Land agitators and suspected them for what they had proved to be. Always a man of direct action, he had not hesitated in his response when they broke in on the meeting. By doing so, he had averted a dangerous and explosive situation. If a single shot had been fired, either at or by the ranchers, Widow's Creek would most likely have become the center of a bloody range war.

"Can you tote this pair to the jailhouse and heave them into the cells, Ottaway?" Smith asked.

"Easy enough," was the reply. "Come on, Stan. You wanted to be a deputy, so you might's well learn all about it."

"Sure, Tal," Jeffreys answered, then he turned his eyes to Smith. "Did you have to treat them this way?"

"I reckon so," the Texan drawled. "And if you're fixing to wear a law badge, don't you-all ever try soft-talking to fellers who smoke that pair's kind of makings."

"How do you mean?" Jeffreys inquired, but he was polite, not arrogant.

"They don't use tobacco," Smith explained. "Likely you've heard of the stuff they use. If you haven't, it's called marijuana."

"Marijuana!" Wil gasped, showing that she for one had heard of it.

"Yes'm," Smith said coldly. "In case you gents don't know what it is, it's a drug that makes yellow-bellied yacks feel like real men. How else do you reckon a stinking pair of soft-shells* like them got up enough guts to come rushing in here *ahead* of the others?"

The time was almost two o'clock in the afternoon. To any chance observer, the two men by the livery barn's big corral had met by accident and were strangers to each other. Leaning against

* Soft-shell: derogatory name for a liberal-intellectual or radical.

the rails, they displayed attitudes of making idle gossip. Their conversation reached no other ears but their own.

"The meeting went off peaceable enough," said the taller of pair. "Give Wax Smith his due, he sure handled them two soft-shells fast and neat."

"That bastard Smith must have a charmed life," complained the smaller man. "First he gets away from Moxley, Hardy and Hayward. Now he's downed the Sheppeys."

"Why the hell did you send *them* after him?"

"We want him out of the way. And I figured that he'd go into the Happy Bull some time this morning. Friendly as he is with Lily Shivers, he shouldn't've been expecting trouble."

"When he saw the Sheppey boys?" the taller man scoffed.

"Did he know them?"

"Well enough to reckon they'd start throwing lead as soon as they set eyes on him. He downed their brother in Arizona and they've been making loud talk about how they'd kill him on sight."

"Damn them!" spat the shorter man. "They didn't mention it to me. At least they both died without talking and Dilkes got away. He says he'll have another go at Smith tonight."

"I wish him luck on it," grunted his companion.

"There's still no word from the men we sent to get C. B. Frith," the small man remarked.

"None," replied the taller, then he stiffened and stared over the other's shoulder. "Nor're we likely to get it."

"What do you mean?" asked the smaller man, turning.

"See that feller in the buggy and leading the *bayo-lobo* hoss?" asked the other man, indicating between the barn's buildings and at the stagecoach trail without making the gesture noticeable except to his companion.

"I see him."

"That's Cedric Burbury Frith."

"Then our men missed him!" croaked the smaller man.

"You can near enough bet he didn't miss them," replied the taller. "Now we'd best get the hell away from here so he doesn't see us together."

11

Settle It Like Men

Wil Jeffreys ought to have been a contented young woman as she walked from her home on Jeffreys Square toward the bank. Due to her forethought, the possibility of trouble flaring up between the ranchers and homesteaders had been reduced if not entirely removed. Faced with the proof that Hopkirk and Woodstole had a legal claim to the C Lazy P land, Bilak had promised that no member of the Grange would try to make homes north of the Elk Fork. Cushman had confirmed the decision, knowing that to do otherwise would give the ranchers a weapon to be used against the Patrons of Husbandry.

Despite some criticism when she had announced her intentions, her insistence on bringing in professional gunfighters to handle law enforcement during the fair had already been justified. She liked and respected Marshal Caster, but doubted if he could have handled the potentially explosive situation as effectively as Smith had when the soft-shells had burst in on the meeting. She wondered if Smith would have shot any farmer who had tried to enter, or fired on Charlie Hopkirk if he had turned before the rancher holstered the Army Colt. Clearly the men concerned had been sure that he would, which was all that mattered.

"Shivery-Shakes, she eats snakes!"

Now why had those words come to her mind? They had been shouted often enough in her childhood and had started many a scuffle with Lily Shivers. Wil sucked in a deep breath and tried to turn her thoughts away from the blonde.

In addition to having once again proved to be as shrewd and capable as any male member of the city fathers, Wil had at last seen her younger brother showing an active interest in civic affairs. After the brief questioning of Smith's behavior, Stanley had helped Ottaway remove the two troublemakers. On his return from the cells in the basement, he had asked if he might serve as a member of the temporary police force. Somewhat to Wil's surprise, Smith had agreed, with the proviso that he work only in the company of a more experienced man and obey orders. Wil regarded Stanley's acceptance of the terms as a sign that he was growing up. Yet she wished that he showed less friendship toward Ottaway.

"Shivery-Shakes, she eats snakes."

Slowly and remorselessly Wil's thought returned to Lily Shivers and the Happy Bull's new sign. No matter how the lady mayor tried to avoid it, she kept remembering the blonde's conditions for refraining from placing it on the saloon.

Damn that Dexter Vendy. Even though he had left Widow's Creek and would never dare to return, his malignant influence was still making itself felt.

Wil and Lily, daughters of the town's founders, had grown up through tomboy childhood and adolescence as friends. Even then Wil had been level-headed and solemn enough to gain the nickname "Chilly Willie," while Lily was always the madcap. There had always been rivalry between them but, until Dexter Vendy had made his appearance, it had never been of a hostile kind. The break between the girls did not come until their return from the Eastern college to which their parents, riding high on the fringe benefits of the cattle industry's boom, had sent them.

Soon after the girls had come home, Vendy had made his appearance. Handsome, dissipated, unscrupulous, he had been in search of an easy life without being burdened by work. Wil, employed in her father's bank, and Lily, even then shocking convention by helping to run the Happy Bull saloon, had each seemed to offer him what he wanted. So he had courted them, while they had vacillated between him and Poona Woodstole.

Thinking back to that period, Wil recalled that Lily had always directed her interest to the man Wil favored. A shrewd judge of character, Wil had seen through Vendy's charm and recognized his motives. There had been an engagement pending. Before it could be confirmed, she had broken it off. Moving in as usual, determined to go one better than Wil, Lily had snapped up his offer of marriage. To the town, it had seemed that the blonde had taken Vendy from under Wil's nose. Even Lily had regarded it in that light.

The marriage had lasted only until the couple reached Chicago on their honeymoon. There Vendy had deserted Lily for an older, richer woman.

All in all, the winter of '86–'87 had had quite an effect on Wil's and Lily's lives. Before the blonde had returned from her desertion, her father, Ben Jeffreys and six more of the town's most influential citizens had perished in the worst blizzard of that terrible season while trying to rescue a snowed-in nester family.

Refusing to accept that the town was finished, Wil had taken over management of the bank and assumed her father's position as mayor. By the sheer force of her driving personality and business acumen, she had brought Widow's Creek through the crisis and toward renewed financial stability. Doing so had not been easy. Although women had been allowed to vote in Wyoming since 1869, most men still regarded running a bank, or being the mayor, as falling solely within the province of males. There had been doubts expressed over whether a beautiful young woman could succeed at either. So Wil had been compelled to take attention away from her looks. Wearing spectacles, keeping her hair in a tight bun and cultivating an expression of chilling, businesslike severity had helped to do it. With Poona Woodstole fully occupied in rebuilding the decimated C Lazy P herds, she had not needed to worry about her looks. Especially as she had no serious rivals with Lily a married woman.

During the period of retrenchment, Lily Shivers—she had stopped using her married name—had become a thorn in Wil's side. The blonde was no longer the gay, carefree girl who had gone away. Probably her treatment since returning had helped bring about the change. Tongues had wagged among the "good" ladies of the town and the pity directed Wil's way earlier had changed to praise for her good sense in seeing Vendy's true character. Maybe

Wil herself had not been tactful on their first meeting, hinting that Lily should have profited by her example in turning Vendy away.

Whatever the cause, Lily had set about running a campaign of harassment and annoyance against Wil. Let her, in her capacity as mayor, organize a function and the blonde would arrange some counterattraction. That new sign was the most blatant and open attempt to humiliate Wil. It could not be allowed. Waxahachie Smith would see that it was not.

"Shivery-Shakes, she eats snakes."

Suddenly Wil realized that she had left her spectacles at home. Not that she needed them. Made of plain glass, they played their part in taking attention from her beauty. However, the change in her appearance did not end there. After lunch, she had let her hair down from its bun. Now it hung free, held back by a dark blue band, as she wore it when riding alone away from the town. She had not changed her clothes, other than adding a pair of thin black leather gloves.

"Why shouldn't a woman be good-looking and efficient?" Wil asked herself.

Surprise showed on the face of a man who was approaching Wil, mirroring the expressions she had seen shown by other people she had passed. He was Lily's head bartender, but greeted Wil warmly, having known her almost as long as his employer.

"Where is Miss Shivers, Alf?" Wil found herself asking.

"Back at the house," the man replied. "She reckoned she'd take a bath and rest up ready for tonight."

"Thank you," Wil said, and went by.

Almost without conscious effort on her part, Wil turned away from the bank. She crossed the street and walked along the alley on the right side of the Happy Bull. At the back of her mind beat one thought. If she wished to retain her self-respect, she could not ask Waxahachie Smith to stop Lily Shivers putting up the sign. It was aimed directly at Wil and she must attend to the matter personally. A smaller voice tried to tell her not to be foolish, but she could neither halt nor turn away from the house where Lily and the saloon girls lived.

"Lily's up in her room," said the pretty blonde who answered

Wil's knock on the front door. Eyeing the lady mayor suspiciously, she went on, "You want to see her?"

"I do," Wil agreed, fighting down a final inclination to retreat.

"Wait here," ordered the blonde. "I'll tell her."

Several more girls gathered in the hall, hostility plain in their attitudes as they glared at Wil. After two minutes, which seemed to drag on interminably, the messenger returned and told Wil to come with her. Entering the Shivers' house for the first time since Lily's return, the mayor found it as clean and neatly kept as when Mrs. Shivers was alive. Going upstairs on the blond girl's heels, Wil felt puzzled by the sight of a wardrobe, dressing table and other furniture standing in the first floor's passage. On being escorted into Lily's quarters, she discovered the reason for it. Only the bed and a thick carpet which covered the whole floor remained in the room.

Clad in a flimsy robe, open to show that she wore nothing but daringly brief, short-legged white lace drawers and black stockings supported by frilly scarlet garters, Lily lounged on the bed. She did not offer to rise, or close her robe.

"I can't offer you a seat," Lily announced. "The rooms' been cleared to redecorate after I've had a rest."

"Can we talk in private?" Wil asked, ignoring the comment.

"Why not?" Lily replied. "Wait outside, Lorna."

"Sure, Lily," the girl replied and left, closing the door.

"Well," Lily said, coming to her feet to stand with hands on hips and naked breasts jutting fully exposed. "What brings you here?"

"You know what," Wil countered, feeling her cheeks redden and guessing that the brazen posture had been adopted to make her blush.

"That new sign of mine?"

"Yes. You know it can't go up."

"Why not? It'll draw me plenty of trade."

"And ruin the fair," Wil pointed out. "If you get away with it, the saloonkeepers across the river will have to come up with something like it and the Lord knows where that will end."

"Hey, look at you," Lily grinned. "Hair down, no glasses. Why, you look almost like a woman."

"Damn it, Shivers!" Wil snapped. "You know a lot of folks have invested their savings in the fair. If it comes off, I can talk the Union Pacific into running a spur line down here. You know what that means."

"That the great Wil Jeffreys, business*man,* has done it again."

"It means prosperity for the town—and for you."

"Maybe I'm happy with the town the way it is," Lily purred. "But I'm an obliging gal. All you have to do is come into the Bull and beg me not to put it up—"

"*Beg* you!" Wil repeated. "I've come to tell you that if you try to put it up, I'll run you out of town."

"You—or Waxahachie Smith?" Lily mocked. "Which of you'll it be, *Mister* Mayor?"

"By God, Shiv—Lily Shivers!" Wil blazed. "I've taken all the riding I aim to from you. It's going to stop."

"Is it, Chilly Willie?" Lily grinned, sensing what the other had almost called her and remembering how Wil had always objected to that name.

"Yes. It is!" Wil answered. "You've been goading and rawhiding me ever since you got back and I've had enough of it."

"Just what do you have in mind?"

"I'm going to do what Dad would have done to any saloon-keeper who'd aimed to put up a sign like that. I'm doing a man's job and so are you. So we'll settle it like men."

"You?" Lily scoffed, watching Wil unbutton the Basque jacket. "Lay one hand on me and I'll scratch your eyes out."

"Maybe you could do it, with those talons," Wil sniffed, sounding a whole lot calmer than she felt. "But you always did like to have the edge."

Up to that moment, if Wil had shown any sign of reconciliation Lily would have accepted it. There was none. Telling the mayor to wait, the blonde stamped by her and into the passage.

"Is Doc Riley in the Bull, Lorna?" Lily demanded.

"I'd be surprised if he's not," the girl replied, watching her employer jerk out a drawer of the dressing table. "What's up?"

"Go tell him to stick around," Lily ordered, and took out a pair of elbow-length black gloves. "And tell the girls not to come up here until I say they can, no matter what they hear."

"Sure," agreed Lorna uncertainly, staring as Lily removed her rings and tossed them into the drawer. "What's—?"

"Go and do it!" Lily commanded. "I'll tell you what it's about tonight."

Watching to make sure that Lorna obeyed, Lily returned to her room and locked the door. Swinging to face Wil, she received a surprise. Not only had the lady mayor taken off her jacket and blouse, but she was removing her skirt.

"I don't want to get my clothes mussed up, or bloody," Wil announced. "And I'd hate to have you wailing that I took an unfair advantage after it's over."

For all her outward calm, Wil felt as if she was boiling inside. Part of her revolted at how she was acting, but more of her demanded that she go on. Months of pent-up anger drove her to meet Lily at the blonde's own level and on even terms. So she continued to undress until all she wore were her knee-long white drawers, stockings and gloves. Shoving her discarded shoes and clothing under the bed, Wil forced herself to turn and face Lily.

"Well, well, well," the blonde said, tossing aside her robe. While drawing on the gloves, she ran her gaze over a bosom as well-developed and waist as slim as her own. "So there is a woman under it after all. It's a pity Poona'll never get to see you like this, Chilly Willie."

Like Lily, Wil would have accepted the slightest hint of a peace offering. The last words warned her that such would not be made.

"I'd say my chances with him are better than yours, Shivery-Shakes," Wil answered. "He doesn't want somebody else's leavings."

"You bitch!" Lily screamed, and flung herself at Wil with hands driving toward the black hair.

That was what the mayor wanted to happen. Ducking under the hands before they could take hold, she rammed two sharp punches against Lily's midsection. With a grunt of pain, the blonde backed off and threw her left at Wil's head. Intercepting the blow with the same ease she had shown in evading Lily's opening attack, Wil again belted her in the stomach. Down went the blonde's hands to cover the point of impact. Like a flash, Wil lunged in and nailed her with a straight left to the cheek, snapping her head around and buckling her at the knees.

"I learned fisticuffs with the Women's Suffrage Movement in college, Shivery-Shakes," Wil warned, watching the other retreat and apparently on the verge of falling.

Gasping, Lily made a grab with her left hand as if to strip off the right's glove. Wil remembered the length of the blonde's fingernails and rushed forward to prevent them being unsheathed. It proved to be a bad mistake. Sidestepping fast, the blonde avoided the charge and drove her bunched left hand into Wil's unguarded right breast. Numbing pain such as she had never experienced ripped through Wil as the knuckles found the sensitive area. She fell back, wide open to the attack with which Lily followed up her advantage. Showing a skill many a man might have envied, the blonde thumped the mayor in the belly and, as she folded over, hooked the other fist into her face to lift her erect. Blood dribbled from the corner of Wil's mouth as she reeled backward into the wall.

"You didn't learn enough," Lily answered, rushing after her like a tigress.

Everything seemed to be revolving wildly before Wil's eyes as she tried desperately to protect herself. Alternating between the mayor's head and body, the blonde kept one blow ahead of her attempts at defense. When Wil tried to cover her head, Lily hammered at her body, either hitting her stomach or jabbing uppercuts at her vulnerable breasts. It was a kind of treatment she had never suffered during "fisticuffs" lessons at college. Soon she careened helplessly the width of the room under the wicked onslaught. It could not last. Taking a roughhouse swing to the jaw, Wil crashed to the floor with a thud that resounded in the room below.

Rolling onto her stomach, Wil made an instinctive attempt to rise. Failing, she sprawled facedown on the thick carpet, her gorgeous, pain-torn body shaking uncontrollably.

Sucking in deep breaths, Lily stood over Wil and watched for any sign that she might be able to get up. After about thirty seconds, Lily hooked her left foot under her shoulder and rolled her onto her back. Still the mayor showed no hint of wanting to resume hostilities.

"Looks like you're all through, big businessman, and I hadn't hardly got started," Lily mocked, then shrugged and turned to walk slowly toward the door. "I'll have Doc Riley come tend your hurts. Any other time you feel like coming to run me out of town, feel free. I'll be pleasured to oblige."

If Lily had looked behind, she would not have felt so complacent. Forcing herself upright, Wil darted after her. While hurt, the mayor had been able to think well enough to know standing when Lily faced her would be dangerous. So she had waited for her chance. The rules learned in the Women's Suffrage Movement's "fisticuffs" classes—taken to prove they could do anything men could—would serve no purpose at that moment. This was not a carefully supervised affair in a boxing ring but a real, anything-goes fight.

Lily's voice smothered the slight sounds made by Wil's feet and the blonde suspected nothing. Even as her right hand reached for the key, Wil caught up with her. Throwing her left arm over Lily's left shoulder, Wil snapped it across the front of her throat in a choke hold. Back and forward flashed the mayor's right fist, pumping and jabbing blows into the saloonkeeper's kidney region. Flattened against the door, Lily could do little or nothing to protect herself. Then Wil heaved with her left arm and twisted around. Thrown off balance and released, the blonde teetered almost to the bed before subsiding onto her rump.

Giving Lily no chance to recover, Wil rushed up. Swooping over, she dug greedy fingers into the long blond hair. A heave brought Lily, squealing protests, almost to her feet. Turning with her back to the blonde, Wil again encircled Lily's throat with the left arm. Having gained the hold, the mayor rained punches into the bewildered girl's head and face.

"I'm ready to start again right now!" Wil gritted as her leather-encased knuckles drew blood from the blonde's nose and lips.

Through the agony of the brain-jolting impacts came a sickening realization that Lily had underestimated Wil's courage and determination. Instead of being beaten, the mayor had tricked her. Now she was paying the penalty for her mistake by taking back as much punishment as she had previously handed to Wil.

Half-strangled as well as receiving the blows, Lily knew that she must try to escape. She was at Wil's mercy and could be sure that none would be shown. Three times she raked the tips of her fingers down the mayor's bare back, clawing at the choking left arm with the other hand. Then she understood why her efforts produced no results. Covered by the gloves, her nails were unable to dig in and rip her way out of the chancery hold.

Sobbing curses, Lily allowed her knees to sag until her sweat-sodden torso rested against Wil's left hip. Thrusting her left arm between the mayor's spread-apart thighs and clamping her right arm tightly about Wil's waist, she surged upright. Wil let out a startled yelp as her feet rose from the floor. Retaining her hold on the blonde's neck, she stopped the pummeling and sank the free hand deep into Lily's hair. In her efforts to throw Wil from her, Lily staggered backward. Still locked together, they tumbled onto the bed.

Such was the force Lily put into her effort that Wil lost her hold as they fell. Passing over the blonde's head, she rolled across the covers and onto the floor. Landing on her derriere, Wil saw Lily wriggle around to follow her. Bouncing from the bed, the blonde landed astride the mayor almost as if trying to sit on her lap. Lily's weight carried over backward. Straddling Wil with her knees, Lily swung slaps and punches at her face. Kicking wildly, but ineffectively, with her legs, Wil tried to catch the hands that flailed at her. Failing, she hurled up a jab that rammed her left fist into the blonde's already bloody nose. Squeaking in pain, Lily grabbed at and caught the wrist before it could withdraw. An instant later their unoccupied palms met and fingers interlocked.

"When I've finished with you," Lily gasped, straining to keep Wil pinned to the floor, "Poona'll look away instead of at you."

Putting all she had into a sudden pitching thrust, Wil toppled the blonde over. Retaining their handholds, the mayor assumed the upper position. With her hips between Lily's thighs and bosom pressed against bust, Wil glared down. Feeling Lily trying to lock her legs around for a scissor grip, she eased up her rump to counter the attempt.

"Don't think he'll even look once at you!" Wil hissed back. "Because I'm going to make you want to leave town."

Releasing the trapped wrist, Lily grabbed for hair and Wil duplicated the move with her left hand. Jerking their other fingers apart, they transferred them to help in tearing at hair. Tight as two lovers, they went rolling along the floor. The nature of the fight had undergone a transformation. All signs of skillful attack and defense were forgotten. With no more definite thought than to inflict punishment on the other girl, they churned and wrestled in a wild, primitive tangle of waving arms and thrashing legs.

For almost three minutes, practically without a pause, Wil and Lily battled in that fashion. They were oblivious of repeated poundings on the door and shrill, excited feminine voices demanding to know what was happening. Screams, gasps and shrieks broke from them as they punched, slapped, nipped, pulled, kneed, kicked or bit mindlessly at each other. Occasionally one of them would shove clear and get to her knees, but the other always tackled and brought her down before she could stand upright. Nor did they stay face to face. Sometimes they would be head to foot, or one on the other's back, or even back to back. Once, wriggling out between the kneeling blonde's thighs, Wil found her face pressed against the other's well-padded buttocks. There was only one thing to do in such a position. Lily screeched aloud as the teeth sank home, and dived away. Later, the blonde returned the treatment as Wil, thrust aside by her feet, fell facedown on the bed. Squealing, Wil reared onto her knees and shoved Lily away from her with such a force that the blonde fell and rolled several feet.

Slowly the girls dragged themselves erect and faced each other. Lily croaked in her attempts to replenish her aching lungs with air, and swayed from side to side in exhaustion. To her amazement and horror, Wil showed no hesitation about returning to the attack. While sweat-sodden, bruised and bloody, now clad only in her tattered drawers, the mayor seemed in better physical shape than the saloonkeeper. That was understandable, for Wil lived an active life which kept her muscles exercised and toned up. Lily followed a more sedentary occupation.

Trailing her one remaining stocking behind her, Lily tried to throw a slap. Wil sprang the remaining distance, thrusting out with both hands. They clapped on the blonde's heaving bosom and shoved hard. So slowly had Lily's arm been moving that her palm missed Wil as she was sent staggering backward across the room. Brought to a halt by the wall, she slumped against it and stared at the approaching lady mayor.

"N—N—No!" Lily sobbed, holding out her left hand weakly. "D—Don't h—"

Instead of continuing her attack, Wil lowered her raised hands. Instantly Lily's right fist hurled upward. Caught under the jaw, Wil spun back several steps and crumpled facedown on the floor. Delighted by the success of her bluff, Lily shoved herself from the wall and advanced. Sinking down, she lay on the mayor's back. Sliding her left arm under Wil's throat, Lily started to choke her and the right's fingers made a determined effort to tear out a hank of the black hair.

Pain blazed through Wil's reeling senses. Croaking out sounds which might have been words, she grabbed Lily's left forearm in both hands and jerked it forward. Down ducked Wil's head and sharp white teeth sank through the black material of Lily's glove into the flesh below. The blonde screeched loud and long. Trying to escape, she eased herself upward above Wil. Releasing the arm with her hands the mayor grabbed over her. Sinking her fingers into Lily's matted, disheveled hair, she hauled down on it. At the same moment, Wil thrust her rump from the floor until she stood on her head and feet. She had made the movements with such speed and power that Lily was catapulted from her. Turning a somersault, the blonde landed on her back and bounced twice.

Wil beat Lily to regaining her feet. While the sobbing blonde was still trying to rise, the mayor reached her. Up hurled Wil's right knee, taking Lily full in the face. Blood gushed in an increasing volume as she was lifted erect and sent blundering away to fall backward onto the bed. The blonde was beaten and knew it. Every inch of her almost naked body throbbed in a white-hot cauldron of torment. Her head felt on the verge of exploding after the knee-kick she had just taken. Through the pain mists which boiled about her, she saw Wil looming above her.

A sense of wild, primitive elation filled Wil. Yet she remembered what had happened when she had last thought the blonde beaten. She did not intend allowing it to happen again. By the time she was through, Lily would be irrevocably licked.

Leaping astride the still conscious but completely impotent blonde, Wil forced both arms against Lily's sides and clamped them there with her knees. That rendered the blonde unable to defend herself, while leaving the mayor's hands free. Going by Lily's expression and feeble attempts to escape, she knew what to expect. Taking her time, Wil let fly with a left that snapped the blond head around as far as the bed's mattress would permit. Across flashed Wil's right fist as soon as Lily's face pointed upward. Then another left, right, left, right, the tempo increasing and the blows pelting the blonde's battered features from side to side. Diluted somewhat by many tears and the sweat pouring from both overheated bodies, Lily's blood soaked Wil's gloves and splattered on the covers. At that moment there was only one thing for which the blonde might have counted herself lucky. Wil was so exhausted that her blows fell at much less than their earlier force.

Swinging around, Wil's right hand missed its mark. She overbalanced and fell from her bosom-cushioned perch. Sobbing in pain and exhaustion, Wil lowered her protesting body from the bed. Slowly she turned to face her rival, hoping that she would not need to continue her exertions. Lily lay motionless, having passed into merciful unconsciousness soon after the final battering had commenced.

All the elation ebbed away from Wil and sanity returned. Dragging feet which seemed to be weighted with lead, she stumbled around the bed and retrieved her clothes. The door crashed open as she was trying to pull on the skirt. Followed by the doctor and some of Lily's girls, Waxahachie Smith burst into the room.

"What the hell?" the Texan said, skidding to a halt.

"See—to—Shiv—Shiv—doctor!" Wil ordered, holding the skirt to cover her naked bust. The room seemed to be rocking and twirling around, but she forced herself to go on. "And one of you girls tell her I want to see her in my office at the bank tomorrow morning. If—she—can make it."

That proved to be Wil's final effort. Letting the skirt fall, she collapsed in a heap and slid limply from the bed.

"What the hell started this?" Lorna inquired, staring in amazement from one battered, bruised and bloody girl to the other but addressing her words to Smith. "Lily told that painter to quit working on the new sign and burn it just after you and Miss Jeffreys left the saloon this morning."

12

An Attorney-at-Law
from Cheyenne

"Wax," Ottaway said, walking into the marshal's office followed by the burly "drummer." "This here's C. B. Frith. I met him putting his hoss up at the livery barn and fetched him along. They said at the bank that Miss Jeffreys won't be in today."

While Smith did not feel surprised at the last piece of information, considering the mayor's condition when he had last seen her, he made no comment on the subject. Instead, he laid aside the sheaf of wanted posters he had been examining and rose from the desk.

"So you're C. B. Frith," Smith greeted, and held out his right hand. "I never did figure you for a traveling salesman for Schuyler, Hartley and Graham."

"I was, way back," Frith objected, his grin matching the Texan's. "And Cedric Burbury's my given names. Only I'd sooner you gents didn't spread that around. There's not many folks knows it."

"Looks like you two know each other." Ottaway commented.

"We met down at Gilpin's," Smith explained sketchily, resuming his seat behind the desk and indicating the room's other chairs. "Pull up and set a spell. You played them close to your vest down there, Ric."

"So did you," Frith pointed out as he seated himself facing the Texan. "I figured you was heading here to be hired, same as me, but I didn't know if the same feller had sent for us both."

"Comes out we're both on the same side, anyways," Smith drawled. "And I can't say I'm sorry over that."

"Or me," Frith replied. "Point being, Wax, who's on the other side?"

"You mean who-all sent those three jaspers to Gilpin's after me?"

"Something like that. There's a heap of this 'sending after' going around. Three fellers tried to put windows in my skull up to Billings."

"Did you get 'em?" Ottaway inquired, having drawn up a chair and perched himself astride it.

"Two're wolf bait," Frith admitted. "But the other was still alive when I left to come down here."

"Did he tell you who'd sent him, Ric?" Smith wanted to know.

"Was hit bad and unconscious," the burly man answered. "I left the Big Indian and Jed Trotter there to see if he'd tell anything when, or if, he come to. Doctor allowed it'd be three, four days at most before they'd know which it'd be. So they'll be here Monday or Tuesday to tell me. Mr. Ottaway here allows that the mayor wants to take on some more men."

"Sure does," agreed Smith. "I was counting on asking you, not knowing you'd already been asked." He looked at the burly man quizzically. "Do you want to cut the cards, or spin a coin for who wears the marshal's badge?"

"You've got it on, so keep it there," Frith replied cheerfully. "Likely there'll not be enough difference in the pay for it to be worth dickering over. I can take orders as easy as giving 'em."

"How about getting more help?" Ottaway demanded.

"If my recommendation's any good, you could do worse than take the Big Indian and Jed when they get here," Frith suggested. "They might not look like churchgoing folks, but they've sand to burn and'll do to ride the river with when the water's over the willows."

Suddenly Smith became aware that two men were standing outside the open door, listening to the conversation. He recognized the mournful-featured bank teller and Stanley Jeffreys. Coming in, they approached the desk.

"Hope we're not interrupting anything special, Mr. Smith," Jeffreys said. "But Ry—Mr. Ryall thought you should know—"

"What about?" Smith asked.

"Counselor Yorck from Cheyenne has been to the bank, demanding to see Miss Jeffreys," the teller answered. "I told him to try at the house as she wasn't in."

"Now why'd you do a mean thing like that?" Smith inquired. "You know that she's in no shape to talk business."

"Yorck's talking for those two soft-shells you had us toss in the pokey," Jeffreys put in. "So Mr. Ryall thought you should know he'd be coming here."

"He's like that, huh?" Smith drawled. *"Gracias,* Mr. Ryall."

"Miss Jeffreys would have wanted you to know," the teller replied. "Now I've done it, I'll be going back to the bank."

"He's not a bad old cuss," Jeffreys commented after the man had left, then looked pointedly at Frith. "I don't think we've met."

"This's Stan Jeffreys, Ric," Smith introduced. "Stan, meet C. B. Frith."

"Mr. Frith," Jeffreys greeted, shaking hands.

"Try 'Ric,'" Frith suggested, studying the badge on Jeffreys's lapel. "You're a deputy, huh?"

"He's learning the ropes," Smith explained.

A tall, lean, well-dressed man of middle age stalked into the office. Sharp-featured, he carried himself in a manner oozing with self-importance.

"Where's the marshal?" he demanded, running cold eyes over the men gathered around the desk.

"You're looking at him," Smith answered, indicating his badge.

"My name is Yorck. I'm an attorney-at-law and I want an explanation of your actions."

"All of them, Counselor, or just some in particular?"

"I want to know why you assaulted and are holding prisoner two law-abiding young visitors to this city!" Yorck elaborated.

"Who d'you mean?" asked Smith innocently.

"Anthony Landers and Philo Wymar," the lawyer answered. "They were with a bunch of farmers who—"

"Them two!" Smith said in carefully simulated understanding. "They kicked open the door of the mayor's meeting room and come busting in on a private meeting like a drunken Sioux headed for a powwow. I did what I did to stop the law being broken."

"They weren't breaking any law!" Yorck protested.

"Were likely to bust the lock on the door, way they opened it. That's damaging civic property and breaking the law. Only that's not what I was thinking about."

"Then what?"

"I was fixing to stop Charlie Hopkirk breaking it, mostly. Which he would've done if he'd throwed lead into one of them fellers."

"But you assaulted *them,* not *him*!" Yorck croaked, seeing a flicker of a grin on Jeffreys's face although none of the other men at the desk displayed emotion.

"I was facing their way and thought it was a good thing to do," Smith said.

"*You* thought—!"

"I *always* think, Counselor. Those pair'd already bust the law, so I stopped them. But, if you ask around, you'll find that I was just as set on stopping Mr. Hopkirk doing it, even and up to killing him if I had to."

"This whole affair—" Yorck began.

"Have you seen these two young fellers, Counselor?" Smith interrupted.

"Well, no. I haven't," the lawyer admitted. "I only learned about their arrest and treatment on my arrival."

"Take the counselor down to see his clients, Mr. Ottaway," Smith ordered, giving Yorck no opportunity to continue. "You'd best go along, Mr. Jeffreys."

"Sure, marshal," Ottaway responded. "It's this way, Counselor."

"Now look here—!" Yorck spluttered, his temper rising at Smith's abrupt dismissal. He was used to more respectful treatment at the hands of peace officers.

"If the counselor doesn't want to go and see them," Smith continued calmly, "you two had best make the rounds. We'll make them tonight, Mr. Frith."

"Just a minute there!" Yorck began.

"While you're over the river, Mr. Ottaway—" Smith drawled.

"Are you refusing to let me see my clients?" the lawyer challenged.

"I'd say I've been trying to get you to do it," Smith countered.

"Only, way folks're boiling into town and us being shorthanded, I can't keep two deputies waiting around the office until you're good and ready to start. That wouldn't be doing the right 'n' legal thing by the good taxpaying citizens of Widow's Creek. Now would it?"

Anger sent a red flush rising through Yorck's pallid cheeks as he forced himself to admit that, despite his legal training, he had been outmaneuvered by Smith. On hearing of the agitators' arrest, he had come along expecting an easy time and no great difficulty in enforcing his will upon the peace officers. Instead, he had been outtalked and forced into a corner. Against Marshal Caster and his deputies, Yorck would have held a powerful weapon. Such tactics would avail him nothing when dealing with the men who stood around the desk. None of them had anything to lose if he should bring pressure to bear and cause their dismissal. So he could only yield and comply with Smith's suggestion.

"Why didn't you hit him with one of those fancy rulings you spout, Wax?" Frith inquired, after Yorck had departed with Ottaway and Jeffreys.

"I only use them on folks who don't know better, but won't be likely to admit it," Smith replied. "You can bet a son of a bitch like him knows every damned law and ruling, federal or local."

"You sure got him all turned about and whichways," Frith stated, grinning with admiration. "Say. Just what kind of game've we got sat in on?"

Hooking a boot up on the desk, Smith told the burly man why Wil wanted them in town instead of her regular officers. Although he felt sure that Frith could be trusted, he made no mention of the display of jewelry which would be arriving. That had been Wil Jeffreys' secret and Smith figured that she should be the one to make the news of it public. One thing was certain. After the fight with Lily Shivers, the lady mayor was in no condition to carry out her duties that day.

"Have you found out who slashed your girths?" Frith inquired.

"Nope," Smith admitted. "Except that it was somebody who didn't want me getting here ahead of him—or her."

"Lily?" Frith suggested.

"It could be. Her and the mayor've one helluva hate for each other," Smith replied. "And I ran into a fuss in her place this morning."

"So Ottaway told me. But the Sheppey boys've been putting word around that they aimed to make wolf bait of you first time seeing. It could've been chance they was in the Bull. Or they might've figured you traveling up with Lily, you'd get good enough friends to go visit her and wouldn't be expecting trouble."

"Like I said, Ric, Lily and Miss Jeffreys hate each other. They locked horns tooth-and-claw this afternoon over a new sign—Hell, no. Lily'd already had that sign busted and burned. So why the hell did they fight?"

"Who won?"

"Miss Jeffreys, looked like," Smith answered. "Only there'd be nothing for them to fight over. Damn it! There're questions that need answers and the two gals who can give them'll not be able to afore morning at the earliest."

"One thing's for sure," Frith said. "Somebody don't want us here. They've tried to gun both you and me down. How about Ottaway?"

"If they have, he hasn't mentioned it to me," Smith replied. " 'Course, him and me've never been what you'd call *bueno amigos.*"

"I wouldn't. I speak only French, German and good old U.S.," Frith replied. "Maybe we should ask him. Trouble is, I'm not sworn in yet."

"I'm taking you on," Smith declared. "But you'll likely have to wait until morning to talk money with Miss Jeffreys."

"What brought Yorck down on us?" Frith inquired, apparently accepting the situation and satisfied that he would find the conditions of employment suitable.

Smith explained about the meeting and the two young men's abortive attempt to disrupt it.

"Up to them, I wondered if either the ranchers or a homesteader had heard about me coming and thought the other side'd sent for me," the Texan concluded. "I don't anymore."

"Or me," Frith admitted. "But those Free Land bastards might not want us around if they aim to make trouble during the fair."

"It's something to think on," Smith agreed. "Would they have the money and means to find out we'd been sent for and hire men to come after us?"

"I don't know about the means. But they'd have the money. There's some rich fellers backing them. Damned if I can see why a feller with plenty of cash ties in with that kind of trash."

"Makes 'em feel like they're doing good for the less fortunate folks, maybe," Smith guessed. "Or they aim to be sure that they're running things if folks like the Free Land bunch should manage to take over. Sounds like the counselor's done talking to his clients."

Stalking into the office ahead of Jeffreys and Ottaway, the lawyer glared indignantly at Smith.

"I wish to state my complete dissatisfaction at the way in which those two young men have been treated!" Yorck announced.

"Mr. Ottaway, can you and Mr. Jeffreys go and make rounds across the river?" Smith asked, without sparing the speaker as much as a glance. "The counselor's clients had them farmers so stirred up that there might be trouble. It'd be best if they saw some law around."

"Yo!" Ottaway answered. "Let's go, Stan."

"What was you saying, Counselor?" asked Smith.

Yorck drew in a deep breath and let it out again before answering, "They, my clients, claim they were assaulted as soon as they tried to walk peaceably into the meeting—"

"It was a *private* meeting," Smith corrected. "And they bust in like crazy men. So I stopped them before real bad trouble could start."

"And what are they being charged with?"

"Nothing."

"Nothing?"

"I wasn't figuring on it. If the doctor finds that they hadn't been driven crazy by that marijuana they was smoking, but was only drunk and acting *loco* through it, I'll leave them sleep it off for the night and turn them loose in the morning."

"But—But—" Yorck croaked.

"It's always been the way," Smith went on. "If a feller gets wild when he's drunk, he spends the night in the pokey and pays for any damage he's caused. Crazy folks, now, no matter how they got that way, they get took off to some place where they can be looked after proper."

"Are you implying that my clients are insane?" Yorck barked.

"I'm no doctor, Counselor," Smith replied. "All I know is that fellers'd have to be drunk, or *loco,* to act the way they did."

"Was I you, Counselor," Frith put in, "I'd go down and ask your clients which they are, crazy or drunk."

Escorting Yorck down to the basement, Smith and Frith stood outside the steel-barred door while he explained the position to his clients. Startled exclamations broke from the two young men when the lawyer warned that a doctor had been asked to come and check upon their sanity.

"That's the most outrageous thing I've ever heard!" blustered the taller of the pair. "Philo and I are as sane as you."

"Then you must've been drunk," Smith drawled. "It's one or the other."

"Not necessarily," Philo Wymar snorted.

"You'll find Doctor Riley at his office, Ric," Smith said calmly. "Go fetch him. And show him those cigarettes we took from this pair afore he makes his examination of them."

Watching the young agitators, Frith could see from their expressions that Smith had won. Deprived of their cigarettes, the two young agitators had already lost their marijuana-induced courage. Back East, the location of their previous troublemaking activities, they had always been supported by lawyers and politicians who could wield influence over the local peace officers. They had no such advantage in Widow's Creek.

Given time to think, the pair could see how their behavior would appear to people who did not sympathize with their lofty ideals. They were all too aware of the revulsion felt by ordinary men and women toward the use of narcotics. Let the local doctor announce in court that they had been smoking marijuana and the jury would find against them without hesitation. While a term in jail might cloak them with an air of martyrdom, neither was willing to make such a sacrifice.

"We'd been drinking and thought it would be a bit of sport to burst in on that meeting," Wymar admitted sullenly. "Now can we go?"

"Not until morning," Smith replied.

"I fail to see why not," Yorck put in.

"Feller don't get over being drunk that quick," Smith answered. "And if I let them loose, what'll I do with some cowhand, or farmer, who gets brought in drunk, then says he's sober and should be let out?"

"These two young gentlemen are hardly in the same class as a drunken cowboy or farmer," the lawyer pointed out.

"All the more reason for holding them, Counselor," Frith commented dryly. "I seem to recall you whooping up a storm in Cheyenne last year 'cause some rich feller's son was let out of the jail and the cowhands he'd been drinking with got held all night. You reckoned then that the law should be the same for everybody, rich or poor."

"We'll let them out if *you* say so," Smith went on, delighted with the information Frith had just given. "I don't know what other folks'll say, though, when they read why I did it in the newspapers."

"Newspapers?" gulped the lawyer, knowing he was trapped.

"Had the feller who runs the *Widow's Creek News* in about the fuss at the meeting," Smith elaborated. "I asked him to come around later and he should be here soon. What do *you* say I should do, Counselor?"

"I think that you young men will have to stay for the night," Yorck declared, avoiding meeting the prisoners' or the peace officers' eyes. "If you aren't released in the morning, I will take action. And I warn you, marshal, that I will report your behavior to the mayor in the morning."

"That's your privilege, Counselor," Smith drawled, feeling sure that Wil Jeffreys could straighten out the matter—if not to Yorck's satisfaction. "Now, if you're all through here, I've got other work to do."

13

The Mayor's Busy Morning

"Miss Shivers to see you, Miss Jeffreys," Ryall announced from the door of the banker's private office.

"Show her in, please," Wil replied.

Wearing her gray traveling costume and hat, instead of the garish dress which had been her attire on other visits to the bank, and with a veil covering her face, Lily Shivers limped into the office. She glanced at the clock on the wall, which showed the time to be nine o'clock, then turned her eyes to the other girl.

Seated at her desk, Wil had her hair down and looked more feminine than was usual during working hours. In fact, she would have been out-and-out attractive but for the marks left on her face by the fight. Studying two eyes which resembled bluepoint oysters peeping out of their shells and other indications, Lily found some faint satisfaction.

"You look a mess," Lily commented, shoving up her veil to expose features even more bruised and swollen. "And, before you tell me, I look worse."

"Sit down, please," Wil said, coldly formal, then looked by the blonde to where her teller stood at the door. "If anybody else wants to see me, I'll not be more than ten minutes."

"Yes, ma'am," Ryall answered and left, closing the door.

"All right," Lily said, sitting down with some care due to the bite she had received on her rump during the wild rolling tangle on the floor. "You licked me. How long do I have before I get out of town."

"Do you want to get out of town?" Wil countered.

"Do I have any choice? You're calling the play."

"As you've pointed out several times, I am a pretty good busi-nessman—"

"So?" Lily challenged.

"Your balance in the bank stands at eleven thousand, six hun-dred and fifty-six dollars and twenty-nine cents—"

"You're sure it's *twenty-nine* cents?"

"Positive," Wil declared. "That makes you the bank's largest individual depositor. As its president, I'd be a fool to let such a valuable account be run out of town."

"How does the mayor feel about it?" Lily challenged.

"As mayor, I know that you pay all your civic taxes promptly, in full and without complaint. I also know that you contribute generously to any worthwhile charities. You run a respectable, clean and well-kept business and your gambling games are hon-est."

"How would you know *that*?"

"I had the Pinkerton Agency's gambling expert brought in to check on them," Wil admitted, and saw the blonde's swollen lips tighten. "Not for personal reasons, I assure you. A certain promi-nent citizen had been losing heavily at your tables and accused you of cheating. I insisted that we learn the truth before taking any action against you."

"So that's why he never went and complained to Bert Caster!" Lily breathed.

"He went, and complained, but I had proof that you ran straight games," Wil replied. "About that new sign of yours?"

"It's gone," Lily told her.

"And was before I came to see you. Damn it, Shivery, what made you do it?"

"I saw that I was losing friends because of it."

"I mean why did you keep riding me?"

"To see if I could get under your hide and make you stop being a lady businessman. All my life folks have said to me, 'Why don't you act more like Wilhemina Jeffreys?' And all along I knew that you was just as much of a roughneck as I am. Only you had enough sense to hide it. You could always get the better of me, Wil. Even when I thought I'd shoved your face in the dirt with Vendy, it came out you'd done the smart thing. And after that son of a bitch deserted me—I'm not shocking you, am I?"

"I'd decided he was a son of a bitch before you did," Wil reminded her.

"Well, after I came back, I just had to lash out at somebody," Lily confessed. "So I picked on you. It was your fault, coming telling me I should have been warned by you throwing him over. Right then, I swore I'd see if there was a woman under it all. Or if there was any of the old Chilly Willie left in you."

"I tossed you in the Elk Fork for calling me that," Wil remarked.

"You came in with me," Lily protested, smiling and cocking her head over so that she could study Wil through her one open eye. "Are we friends?"

"There's nothing I'd like better," Wil said sincerely. "Except for one thing, that is."

"What?"

"If you try to get your claws into Poona Woodstole, Shivery-Shakes, what I did to you yesterday will be only the start of it."

"By the Lord, Chilly Willie," Lily repeated, grinning as well as her swollen lips would let her. "I do believe you mean it."

"You'd better not forget it, or you'll damned soon find out whether I do or not," Wil warned, also smiling. "By the way. If you can hobble that far, how about coming to my place for dinner tonight?"

"Will Stanley approve?" Lily asked.

"I think he's changing for the better," Wil answered. "He was working with Mr. Smith and the deputies all day yesterday and this morning he'd left for the marshal's office before I got up."

"About time, too," Lily sniffed. "If I come, do I need to bring a pair of gloves?"

"Only if you've got any notions about trying to rub my face in the dirt with Poona," Wil told her. "Because, Shiver, I know *he's* worth having."

"That figures. You've started dressing like a gal again now I'm free to go after him."

"Will you come?"

"I might as well. Do you reckon I dare go into the Bull looking like this and after you licked me? Damn it, Wil, you near on bust my head. For a prim and proper business*lady,* you sure fight dirty."

"So do you. I can hardly sit down, the way you bit my butt end."

"I know just how you feel," Lily sympathized, moving on the chair in an attempt at relieving the pressure on her injury. "Haven't we been fools, Wil?"

"Bloody fools, as Poona would say," Wil agreed, trying to smile. "You'll come tonight?"

"I'll be around at seven," Lily confirmed. "That'll give us time to have a long talk. And if I can do anything at all to help you bring off the fair, you've only got to tell me."

"I will, you can count on it," Wil declared and glanced at the clock. "Now, Miss Shivers, I have work to do. We don't all start in the middle of the afternoon."

"And we don't all finish at four o'clock, Miss Jeffreys," Lily pointed out cheerfully. "Wil—"

"Yes, Lily?"

"Don't you worry about Poona and me. That damned sign ruined any little chance I might have had."

With that, Lily rose and walked slowly and stiffly toward the door. Opening it, she paused and looked back.

"Wil, do you recall a gambling man who came to see you the day I left town?"

"Yes."

"Wax Smith's going to be asking you about him," Lily warned, and walked out of the office without enlarging upon her statement.

Wil was not granted an opportunity to ponder the cryptic utterance. As the blonde departed, Ryall walked in.

"Counselor Yorck wishes to see you, Miss Jeffreys," the teller said, in a tone which showed his feelings about the visitor. "Marshal Smith and Mr. Frith are here, too."

"Has Counselor Yorck said why he wants to see me?"

"Only that it's in your capacity as mayor."

"Then ask them all to come in, please," Wil said, having heard from her brother of how Smith had dealt with Yorck and the agitators.

"Yes, ma'am. Er, will it be all right if I leave the bank for a short time?"

"Of course."

"I've something to attend to at home. It won't take more than half an hour."

"You don't need to explain, Mr. Ryall." Wil smiled. "Show the gentlemen in and then go."

Withdrawing, Ryall stood aside to let the lawyer, Smith and Frith enter. The teller closed the door as the three men approached Wil's desk. From his scowl, Yorck did not care for the other two being present. His opening words made that even clearer.

"I wished to see you in private, Miss Jeffreys," York declared. "Is it necessary for these men to be present?"

"That depends on you," Wil replied, and her normal business attitude had returned. "I believe that you wish to lay a complaint against Marshal Smith and his deputies. In which case, I consider that they have every right to hear and answer it. Bringing them in saves all our time."

"Very well!" Yorck growled. "I have come to state my complete dissatisfaction with this man's," he indicated Smith, "behavior."

"In what respect?" Wil inquired.

"Yesterday they arrested two young men of good family and held them in jail all night."

"With your permission, Counselor," Smith pointed out, "after they'd admitted to being drunk and raising a fuss for the hell of it."

"It was merely a foolish prank—" Yorck boomed.

"And has been treated by Marshal Smith as one," Wil replied. "Despite the fact that it might easily have caused a tragedy. I don't need to tell you, Counselor, just how delicate the situation is between the ranchers and the homesteaders. So I called a meeting between the leaders of both sides to work out an amicable settlement. Those two young men's drunken prank might have ruined our chances of doing it. Mr. Smith acted in a manner which met with my complete approval."

"He might have crippled one of my clients for life."

"And your clients could easily have caused men to be killed," Wil countered. "The way they broke into my private office gave the marshal no choice but to take the drastic measures. I will repeat that he acted in a manner which has my complete approval."

"Do you know that your marshal is a wanted man?" Yorck demanded.

"Only if I go back to Texas," Smith corrected. "And get caught there."

To placate the Mexican government, without yielding to its demands, the Governor of Texas had agreed that Smith would be arrested and handed over if he should be caught within the boundaries of the Lone Star State.

"I know all about that," Wil told the lawyer. "And I am satisfied that Mr. Smith is an honest, respectable member of the community. Yesterday, his prompt action averted a dangerous situation. If you wish, he will rearrest the two young men and bring them to trial on a charge of inciting to riot—"

"While under the influence of drugs," Smith went on.

"That won't be necessary," Yorck answered stiffly. "I came here to lodge a protest and have done so. What action you see fit to take is your concern, Miss Jeffreys."

"You may rest assured that I will deal with it," Wil replied. "Is there anything more, Counselor?"

"Nothing," the lawyer answered. "Good morning."

"There goes a man I could easy get to dislike," Frith commented as the door closed behind Yorck.

"Don't sell him short," Wil warned. "He has some influence in Cheyenne and we may hear more of this affair. I'm sorry, Mr. Frith, but we haven't had time to be formally introduced."

"I fetched Ric along for you to swear him in," Smith remarked, after performing the introduction. "He made the rounds with me last night, but he still needs a badge. Your brother and Ottaway are going around collecting them from Bert's boys."

"How is Stanley shaping up?"

"Raw, but willing to learn, ma'am. It's none of my never-mind, but you could do worse than have him kept on after we've gone."

"He certainly doesn't show much aptitude for banking," Wil

smiled. "I'll be pleased to swear Mr. Frith in, but I think he would like to talk terms first."

"Yes, ma'am," Smith grinned. "I reckon he would. I'll wait outside until you're through. Then, if you can spare the time, there's things to be talked about."

Across the river, the tall and the short man met outside the office of the *Widow's Creek News.* Again, to a casual observer, their coming together would have appeared accidental and their only mutual interest to be the poster in the window giving details of the fair.

"I can't stay long," said the taller.

"Do they suspect you?" asked the other.

"There's no reason why they should, after yesterday," the taller man stated. "But I'd sooner not take chances."

"Have you learned when they arrive?"

"Not yet. But something else's come up."

"What is it?"

"Smith and C. B. Frith are friends," warned the taller man, pointing at the poster as if indicating something on it.

"I know that already," growled the shorter. "It's why Dilkes didn't try to kill Smith last night. They were covering each other all the time they made the rounds and he daren't make a move."

"Frith got one of the fellers we sent after him—"

"Alive?" demanded the shorter man worriedly.

"Just about. He's unconscious, or was when Frith left Billings. Two of his sidekicks stayed behind to see if the bastard can tell anything when he recovers. They'll be down here by Monday or Tuesday and, way I heard it, Smith's going to have them appointed as deputies. Frith reckoned they're real good."

"And they'll be here by Monday?"

"Or Tuesday. Losing Hardy, Moxley, the Sheppeys and the others leaves us hellish shorthanded. Can we get more help?"

"I don't know. If not, we may have to change our plans."

"In what way?" asked the taller man.

"There's not time to go into it now," replied the other. "We've been stood here together as long as's safe."

"Yeah," agreed the taller of the pair. "I'll meet up with you tonight, if I've learned anything. Or tomorrow at the same time, be around the livery barn."

Turning on his heel, the taller man strolled off in the direction of the river. With a similar attitude of nonchalance, his companion stood for a short time looking at the poster. Then the small man glanced in a calculating manner after the other and hurried away in the opposite direction.

Although Smith had hoped for a lengthy discussion with Wil and to have her answer some of the questions which troubled him, the chance did not arise. Almost as soon as he had been called in and informed that Frith had accepted the mayor's offer, Ryall's assistant knocked and entered. One of the bank's most influential depositors had arrived, asking for an urgent interview. Apologizing, Wil had asked the Texan and Frith to excuse her and promised that she would be available for a conference after lunch.

Leaving the bank, Smith had decided that he would take his saddle to be repaired. Requesting that Frith should attend to things at the office, he had gone to the Simple Hotel and collected it. According to the desk clerk, the saddler's shop was on Shivers Street, across the river. So Smith set off in that direction.

Approaching the river, Smith saw Ryall crossing the upper of the three bridges which connected the twin parts of the town. A startled, almost guilty expression flickered across the teller's face at the sight of the marshal and he hurried by without doing more than nod a greeting.

"Hey, Marshal Smith!" yelled a voice.

Going across the bridge, Smith met Jeffreys on the southern bank. The young man wore his suit, a Stetson and town boots, but had on a gun belt carrying a Colt Civilian Model Peacemaker in a fast-draw holster.

"Something up?" Smith inquired.

"No. I went to collect a couple of badges from deputies who live up this end of town. Tal Ottaway's gone for the others."

At that moment, the crack of shots rang out; first one, then two more in rapid succession, followed by the scream of a man in agony. Jeffreys spun around and drew his Colt with both speed and capable efficiency.

"Down by the livery barn!" the young man snapped.

"Let's go!" Smith barked, having removed his glove and fetched out his Colt.

Guided by Jeffreys, Smith ran in the direction of the disturbance. The two peace officers went around to the rear of the livery barn. Pushing through the small knot of onlookers, they went to where Ottaway, still holding his smoking revolver, knelt by a still figure.

"What happened?" Smith asked, holstering his Colt.

"I'm damned if I know," Ottaway answered, and he seemed to be struggling to conceal anger, or some other violent emotion. "I'd come by this way to see if you or Ric was with your hosses and Di —that son of a bitch threw lead at me."

"You know him?" Jeffreys inquired, staring down at the two holes in the figure's forehead.

"His name's Dilkes," Ottaway replied. "I've seen him around town."

"I've done more than that," Smith said quietly. "He's the *hombre* who was with the Sheppeys when they tried to kill me."

14

The Return of the Joneses

"Thing is, Miss Jeffreys," Smith said, as he and his deputies sat with the lady mayor at the table in the room where the two ranchers had met the representatives of the Grange. "Since you hired us, Ric, Ottaway and me've each had somebody try to kill us."

"You, Mr. Frith?" Wil said, turning to the burly man.

"Up in Billings," Frith agreed and explained the circumstances.

"And the Sheppey brothers tried to kill you in the Happy Bull, Mr. Smith," Wil went on. "Then it wasn't just because of their old grudge?"

"I never thought it was, ma'am," Smith declared. "You see, three other fellers tried it at Gilpin's way station."

"Who were they?"

"A gambling man and two more *pistoleros.*"

"The gambler who visited me at the bank?"

"Why'd you think that, ma'am?" Smith demanded.

"Lily gave me a warning, indirectly, that you might be interested in him," Wil explained. "He came to see me to ask about opening a gambling concession during the fair."

"If that feller I dropped was with the Sheppeys, they're all tied in to the gambling man," Ottaway commented.

"I'd say that's likely," Frith admitted dryly. "Somebody doesn't want us as your special police force, Miss Jeffreys. And I, for one, 'd like to know who."

"And why," Smith drawled.

"What do you think, Mr. Smith?" Wil inquired.

"I'm da—don't know, ma'am," the Texan replied. "There's some's'd say Lily Shivers would make a good one for 'who.' "

"Why should she want to stop you gentlemen arriving?"

"What happened yesterday between you and her could answer that."

"I don't think so, Mr. Smith. Lily had what she regarded as a personal grudge against me. All her escapades have been directed my way, not at the town. She'd even had that sign destroyed when she saw how P—how people regarded it. Widow's Creek is Lily's home and she's a shrewd enough businesswoman to see the advantages a successful fair will bring."

"You trust her, then, ma'am?" Frith asked.

"I'm inclined that way," Wil agreed.

"Would the ranchers, Woodstole and Hopkirk, try to stop us, figuring we'd been hired by the nesters?" Frith went on.

"That's most unlikely. Poo—Mr. Woodstole has been working with me to organize the fair and it was he who suggested hiring Mr. Smith."

"Woodstole!" Smith exclaimed. "Now I remember. Her name was something Woodstole afore she married Captain Fog."

"Beagrave-Woodstole," Wil supplied. "She's Poona's cousin."

"Who put up the rest of us, ma'am?" Frith put in.

"I hired Mr. Ottaway," Wil explained. "In fact, it was meeting him which gave me the idea of bringing in gunfighters—I hope the term doesn't offend you?"

"We've all been called worse," Smith drawled. "How about the others?"

"I'd heard Mr. Frith's name mentioned and knew that he was running the marshal's office in Billings. So I sent for him. Mr. Ottaway recommended Seaborn Tragg and Frank Straw."

"Could be the Free Land crowd didn't want us around," Ottaway remarked. "If they aim to stir up fuss, it'd be easier and safer against Caster's deputies than us."

"Why would they want to do it?" Wil asked.

"To rub the Grange's face in the dirt," Smith suggested. "Show the farmers that the Free Land crowd are more concerned with their interests than the Grange are. A play like that'd be their way."

"Disrupting the fair would embarrass the Grange," Wil agreed.

"It would also stir up trouble between the cowhands, who're looking forward to a week's celebrations, and the farmers."

"Yes'm," Smith drawled. "Then it'd be the usual story back East. Drunken cowhands terrorizing the community and abusing the poor, hardworking, God-fearing homesteaders."

"I'll concede that the Free Land Society would be capable of acting as you suggest," Wil said. "But do you think that's what is behind the attempts on your lives?"

"Would they be able to learn who you'd sent for, or who'd accepted?" Smith wanted to know.

"I never kept the fact that I was hoping to hire you gentlemen a secret," Wil replied. "If they'd planned their campaign well in advance, they could have found out, I suppose."

A knock on the main door prevented Smith from raising the matter of the jewelry. It opened and Marshal Caster entered.

"Wax!" he said. "I thought you should know. The Jones brothers're back and down at the Busted Plow."

"So?" Smith asked.

"There's still a warrant on them for slow-elking,"* Caster elaborated. "We didn't send it after them. But it'll have to be served now they're back. And fast."

"How come?" Frith asked.

"Some of the C Lazy P boys're in town," Caster explained. "If they hear the Joneses're back, it'll be the same as throwing a lit match into a keg of black powder."

"That's for sure," Jeffreys agreed. "The hands were riled when Poona wouldn't let them fetch them back after they'd run out."

"Let's go, boys!" Smith snapped. "Where's the warrant, Bert?"

"In the office safe," Caster replied. "Come on, I'll find it for you."

Without wasting more time in discussion, Smith led the other men from the room. On reaching the marshal's office, Caster went to the safe and opened it. Smith crossed to the wall rack and took down his rifle, which he had brought from the hotel that morning.

"Get loaded for bear," the Texan told his deputies. Frith and

---

* *Slow-elking:* butchering and selling cattle.

Ottaway selected twin-barreled shotguns, but Jeffreys stood by the desk. "You too, Stan."

"But—!" the young man began, making a gesture toward his holstered Colt.

"I don't want trouble taking them," Smith went on.

"Then why take the shotguns?" Jeffreys asked.

"That's to make sure we don't have any," Smith explained.

"Here's the warrant," Caster announced, joining Smith and handing over a legal document. "If you need any help—"

"I reckon we can handle it, Bert," Smith replied. "This's the kind of thing Miss Jeffreys hired us to do."

Caster nodded in gratitude. While he would have performed his duty, arresting the Jones brothers might have antagonized the other farmers. If it did under the present circumstances, their antipathy would be directed against Wil Jeffreys's imported peace officers and not at Caster and his men.

With the warrant in his hip pocket and rifle under his arm, Smith led the deputies, each carrying a shotgun, out of the town hall. Following them out, Caster nodded again, with satisfaction. Clearly Smith knew his way around the town, for he was taking the most direct route to the Busted Plow saloon.

Making his way across the river, Smith wondered if they might be going to face the reason for the attempts on their lives. Smith and Caster had been unable to trace the Sheppey brothers' companion after his escape from the Happy Bull. So he could have been hidden in town, or maybe left on foot. There were farms within easy walking distance where he and the Sheppeys might have hidden while awaiting their chance to kill Smith.

Nor, if he knew anything about their kind, would the Free Land Society's organizers hesitate to use violence to achieve their ends. If they planned agitation and incidents to disrupt the county fair and gain publicity for their schemes, they would not hesitate about trying to kill anybody who stood in their way.

Having crossed the center bridge, the peace officers made their way along Shivers Street. The main business section south of the river, the street had two saloons on its length. Near the river was the Brand Book, haunt of the cowhands. Closer to the edge of town and on the opposite side stood the farmers' gathering place, the Busted Plow. Several horses which looked more suitable for light haulage than full-time saddle work stood at the hitching rail of the Busted Plow.

A cowhand was riding toward the Busted Plow, instead of making to where a half-dozen cow ponies awaited their masters' pleasure outside the Brand Book. Dismounting, he fastened his reins to the hitching rail. Then, with Smith and the deputies increasing their pace, he strolled into the farmers' saloon. The batwing doors had barely swung outward behind him when a rifle cracked and he reeled out again clutching at his chest.

"Hit the side door, Ric, Ottaway!" Smith barked, sprinting toward the building. "Stan. See to the cowhand."

Breaking away from his companions, Frith ran along the alley toward the nearer side's door. Ottaway dashed on, turning at the other end of the saloon. Following Smith, Jeffreys dropped to one knee beside the wounded cowhand and rested his shotgun against the end support of the hitching rail. The Texan went on to the sidewalk with a bound, crossed it and thrust open the doors. Landing on spread-apart feet, rifle held ready for instant use, Smith swung a quick gaze around the room. The rear door swung closed. At the bar stood two men who were enough alike to be twins. Behind the counter and scattered about the room, the bartender and several customers stood in strained, worried postures. Smith's eyes went back to the possible twins. They had the appearance of farmers, yet wore gun belts and carried revolvers in fast-draw holsters. Neither of them had a rifle, but the one on the right held a revolver which he slanted in Smith's direction.

Not for long. Flying open, the left side door admitted C. B. Frith behind a shotgun. Across the room, Ottaway came in equally ready for trouble.

"Drop the gun, *pronto*!" Smith commanded.

Cold, suspicious eyes glared at Smith. As always when carrying out the duties of a peace officer, he looked clean and tidy. Smith had never heard of psychology, but practical experience had taught him that an appearance of cleanliness and neatness impressed people more than a slovenly aspect. However, the brothers did not like what they saw. Apart from his boots, Smith might have been a cowhand or a reasonably prosperous rancher. He was certainly a Texan, hailing from a state with its very roots buried in the cattle business.

No matter how they might regard Smith personally, the brothers knew better than refuse to obey. So the one holding his revolver twirled it flashily and returned it to his holster.

"Round the back, Mr. Ottaway," Smith requested. "The one with the rifle's gone that way."

"Yo!" Ottaway replied, and left the room.

"Who're you?" asked the second of the brothers sullenly.

"Name's Smith. I took over marshal yesterday."

"Marshal!" spat out the first brother. "They didn't say not—"

"Shut your mouth!" barked the second, then swung his gaze around at the other customers. "Are you going to let these cattlemen's John Laws take us?"

"They are," Smith stated. "You don't figure they're going up against shotguns to save your hides. Even without the other."

"What other?" demanded the second brother.

"Article Eleven, Section Twenty-Three, Item Sixty-One of the Wyoming Criminal Justice Code," Smith elaborated, watching the farmers rather than the brothers. "It says, any man who offers succor and assistance to a wanted person whereby the said person escapes arrest will be taken into custody and held until said person is captured. So you gents just carry on with whatever you was doing while I arrest the Joneses for slow-elking."

"Slow-elking," gulped the first brother, seeing no sign of support among the other customers. "So that's why you're here!"

"Neither of you's got a rifle," Smith drawled. "So it couldn't've been you who shot the cowhand. I'll get round to that when my deputy comes back."

The left side door opened and Ottaway returned on his own.

"He got away, marshal. They'd got three hosses out back and he took off with all three of them. Was too close to houses or people for me to cut loose with a scatter or handgun."

"All right, you pair," Smith said. "Shed those gun belts, *pronto.*"

"We didn't shoot him," Morgan Jones said, looking uneasy.

"Like I said," Smith answered. "I'm arresting you on that slow-elking warrant you run out from."

"Marshal!" Jeffreys called, standing up on the sidewalk and speaking over his shoulder without taking his attention from the street. "I think you'd best come out here."

"I'm coming," Smith replied, guessing why the request had been made. "Take over here, Ric."

"Yo!" Frith answered. "Get them gun belts shed and fast!"

There was a quiet, deliberate menace in the burly man's voice which caused the brothers to obey. Unbuckling their gun belts, they let the weapons slip to the floor and stood glowering after Smith as he headed toward the door.

As he crossed the room, Smith could see what was going on outside. Two cowhands had arrived and Jeffreys stood facing them. Before Smith reached the door, the young deputy turned away from the pair and started to point along the street. Like a flash, the taller of the pair lifted up a Colt revolver and slammed its barrel against the back of Jeffreys's skull. Although the Stetson took some of the impact, Jeffreys stumbled to his knees. Ignoring his companion, who had dropped to kneel by the shot man, the cowhand charged through the batwing doors.

Down swung Smith's Colt rifle, its foregrip slide flashing to the rear and staying there. The cowhand skidded to a halt, eyes flaring widely as they looked into the muzzle of the rifle. Then he swung his gaze by Smith and halted it on the Jones brothers at the bar.

"Get off of my trail, marshal!" the cowhand ordered.

"That's not what I'm hired and paid to do, friend," Smith replied gently.

"I don't want to kill you, marshal," the young cowhand warned. "But I'll do it to get at them pair of bastards for what they done to Alvin."

"Thing for you to figure on," Smith said in the same even tone, "is if you want to kill them enough to die for doing it."

"Huh?"

"You can only do it after I'm dead. And you can't kill me without taking lead yourself."

The cowhand's Colt lined just as squarely at Smith's chest as the rifle's barrel pointed his way, its trigger depressed and the hammer retained at full cock by his thumb. Nobody else in the room made a move. Although Frith threw a quick look at Smith, he kept his shotgun lined on the brothers. Ottaway turned and his ten gauge's twin tubes circled the farmers in an all-embracing, menacing gesture. For his part, Smith stood as if made of stone and his eyes stayed on the cowhand's face, forcing the other to meet his gaze.

"How do you mean?" asked the cowhand.

"Look at this rifle I'm pointing at you," Smith advised. "It's not like any you've seen, likely. As soon as my left hand loosens on the foregrip, it'll go forward and fire. So, even if you shoot me, you'll die right after."

"I don't want to shoot you!" the cowhand protested. "It's them Joneses—"

"Neither of them shot your *amigo.*" Smith interrupted. "Take my word on it. Now put up your gun and leave me find out who did."

"Leather it, Robbie!" ordered Poona Woodstole's voice from outside the saloon. "Go on. Put it away. It won't solve anything."

"That's real sound advice, cowboy," Smith confirmed, having been giving so much of his attention to Robbie that he had not noticed the rancher's arrival. "You don't want to kill me, or them."

"Alvin's dead!" Robbie groaned, lowering the revolver.

"We'll get the man who killed him," Smith promised, taking his rifle out of alignment. "And when we do, it'll be the right one."

Then the Texan walked by Robbie. Rubbing his head, Jeffreys came into the room after Woodstole. The young deputy looked anxious and miserable as he met Smith's questioning gaze.

"It was my own fault, Wax," Jeffreys declared. "I looked away when Robbie said Poona was coming."

"You'll know better next time," Smith guessed. "Take him to the jailhouse and put him in a cell."

"Jail!" Robbie yelped. He had turned as Smith went by and started to holster his revolver.

"You pistol-whipped my deputy," Smith replied. "That can't be overlooked. And, if you reckon I was kidding about my rifle—"

With that, Smith released the foregrip. It rode forward, feeding a bullet from the tubular magazine into the chamber. With the trigger portion of the action removed, there was nothing to hold back the hammer and it slammed home to ignite the primer. Flame belched from the barrel, which he had angled upward above the batwing doors, and the bullet winged off over the opposite building. Almost before the sound of the shot had died away, Smith pivoted to face the cowhand.

"Trouble being," the Texan drawled, "I have to fire it every time I pull back the slide."

"Go with Deputy Jeffreys, Robbie," Woodstole ordered, knowing that Smith could not do other than arrest the cowhand. "I'll help you get things straightened out with the marshal."

"Sure, boss," Robbie answered. "How about Alvin?"

"I'll see to him," the rancher promised.

"Ric," Smith called. "Take the Joneses down to the jail. Put them in a cell away from the cowhand. If they want a law-wrangler, see that they get one."

"Yo!" replied the burly man. "What'll you be doing?"

"Finding out just what did happen here," Smith said grimly. "See my deputies get by the cowhands, Mr. Woodstole. Then I don't reckon any of these gents will object if you come back and hear what they have to say."

"Just remember, us Joneses are farmers like you!" Morgan yelled. "We're on your side—"

"But I'm not on yours when it comes to murder!" barked a dour-faced old man in a tone that suggested Scottish birth. "And that's what's been done this day."

Giving the brothers no time to continue their arguments, Frith and Ottaway forced them to leave the saloon. Woodstole followed them, speaking to the small knot of cowhands who had gathered on the street. It said much for the respect earned by the Englishman that the cowboys accepted his order to let the Joneses pass. Arranging for the body to be taken to the undertaker's shop, Woodstole returned to the barroom. Smith was placing his rifle on the counter and looking around.

"What happened?" the Texan asked the bartender, picking up the Jones brothers' discarded gun belts.

Being part owner of the Busted Plow, the bartender drew most of his trade from the farmers. So he hesitated and looked around at his customers as if seeking guidance. The dour-featured Scot rose and approached the bar.

"It was deliberate, cold-blooded murder, marshal. The Jones boys must've seen Alvin ride up, they were stood with their backs to the bar. I saw Evan say something to the other two. Then, as soon as Alvin walked in, Evan whipped up his rifle and shot him."

"Why'd a cowhand come in here?" Smith asked.

"He's going with Joe Gladwin's daughter," another farmer answered.

"Evan had no reason to shoot him," the bartender went on. "Alvin's been in here plenty of times and never caused any trouble. He didn't make a move toward his gun, but Evan upped with his Ballard and shot him."

"I reckoned what he did surprised his brothers," the Scot continued. "But Morgan threw down on us and Virgil told Evan to get out the back way and leave town as fast as he could."

"I don't think they was expecting the law to arrive so soon," the bartender remarked. "It all happened so fast, there wasn't a thing I could do, marshal."

"Where's Evan now?" Woodstole asked, and his normally languid air had left him.

"He got away," Smith replied. "But I'll find him and fetch him back."

"You'd better, Wax," the Englishman warned quietly. "Charlie's at Wil's office with Cousin Basil and he's going to take a whole heap of calming down when he hears what's happened to young Alvin."

"Likely," Smith answered. "But you'd best do it, Poona. If you don't, I'll have to. And I'll do it any way I need."

15

An Ultimatum for Smith

To say that Charlie Hopkirk was angry when he heard of Alvin's death could almost be called the understatement of the decade. On learning that the killer had escaped, the old rancher had sworn that he would gather every cowhand in Wyoming Territory and search every farmhouse until he found Evan Jones. Backed by Wil Jeffreys, Poona Woodstole had finally succeeded in quieting Hopkirk down. Not only that, but Zorin Bilak had arrived to offer all the help the Grange could arrange in running down and apprehending the killer. So Hopkirk had agreed to take no action, provided Evan Jones was brought in for trial.

For almost an hour, Smith had expected a range war to blow up. Diplomatically he and his deputies had taken no part in the calming of the old rancher. With that matter settled, at least for the time being, the peace officers had been faced with the problem of guarding Sir Basil Houghton-Rand's collection of jewelry. Fortunately, most of that work had been taken off Smith's hands. The insurance company had insisted on employing the Pinkerton Agency to guard the collection. One of their precautions had been to throw a cloud of secrecy over the affair. Even the date of their arrival had not been announced and the telegraph message received by Woodstole had deliberately been wrong. Except when on display, the collection would be kept in the bank's safe and one of the four agents was to be constantly on guard. Due to the urgency of the situation, Smith had not gone further into the matter of added protection. The jewelry would remain in the safe until after the fair had been declared open on Monday. So he had promised to hold a conference with the Pinkerton men during the weekend and make the necessary arrangements.

The meeting had been held in Wil's office at the bank. On returning to the jail, Smith had found Yorck waiting. Apparently the Jones brothers were the lawyer's clients and he had insisted on being present when Smith interviewed them. After asking if Jeffreys felt fit to work, and being assured that he did, the Texan had sent him and Ottaway onto the streets. Then he and Frith accompanied Yorck to the basement cells.

On being questioned, the brothers had insisted that Alvin had started to draw on them as soon as he entered the Busted Plow. Virgil did most of the talking and had declared that he did not know where Evan might be. When asked why Evan had fled, Virgil had claimed that his brother doubted if he would get a fair trial in Widow's Creek, but was willing to give himself up to the authorities at Cheyenne or Laramie. Knowing that he would learn no more with the lawyer standing by, Smith had ended the interview. The Texan had told Yorck that he was holding the brothers on the old slow-elking warrant and also as material witnesses to the killing, so he would oppose the granting of bail. Although the lawyer had blustered, he knew that the local justice of the peace would back Smith on the matter. So Yorck had contented himself with promising to return at regular intervals and "protect his clients from abuses."

There had been only one reasonably bright spot in the whole afternoon and evening for Smith. By the time his various duties had been completed, sundown was so close that he could do little more than find the general direction by which Evan Jones had left the town. However, a telegraph message had reached Frith from his two companions. The wounded man had died without speaking, but the Big Indian and Jed Trotter would reach Widow's Creek by Monday. So Smith would have the extra help he needed during the fair. That piece of news had been greeted with relief by Jeffreys and Ottaway when they had heard it.

The night had passed without incident. Cowhands and farmers stayed away from each other while Smith and his deputies had patrolled until the town showed signs of having gone to sleep.

Leaving Ottaway and Frith at the office, Smith had spent the rest of the night in his room at the Simple Hotel. Next morning, clean-shaven and tidy, he had arrived at the office to find Wil Jeffreys and Lily's head bartender there with his two men.

"Something's happened to Lily, Wax," Frith announced. "She didn't go back to the house last night."

"She left me just after midnight," Wil went on. "I hoped that Stanley would be home in time to escort her, but he stayed here—"

"No, ma'am," Frith interrupted. "He didn't stay here."

"That's right, Miss Jeffreys," Smith confirmed. "He came off with me around midnight and said he was headed for home."

Before any more could be said, Counsellor Yorck walked into the office with a sheet of paper in his hand.

"This was pinned to the front door of my host's house, marshal. I thought that I had better bring it along."

Taking it, Smith opened it and started to read aloud.

"Warning. If the Jones brothers, falsely imprisoned at the insti-gation of the ranchers, are not released by sundown today, Lily Shivers and Stanley Jeffreys will be killed. The Friends of Justice."

"Well?" Yorck asked.

"I didn't know Lily and young Stan were missing," Smith drawled. "Somebody's running a bluff."

"Is your brother at home, Miss Jeffreys?" Yorck asked. "I say this because I have heard about this despicable organization called the Friends of Justice. They took hostages in another town. When their demands weren't met, they killed the hostages and took an-other two the next night."

"So you're saying we should do like the note says, Counselor?" asked Smith.

"I am merely pointing out the danger," Yorck protested. "This matter could prejudice my clients' chances if they are brought to trial, so naturally I am interested in what happens."

"Maybe they'd best hear about this," Smith suggested. "You allowed that you wanted to be on hand every time we questioned, or talked to, your clients, so you'd best come along."

"Very well," Yorck grunted. "I'll come."

Going to the basement, Smith read the message to the Jones

brothers. Although Virgil showed no emotion, Morgan grinned triumphantly at Wil, the deputies and Yorck. Clearly the younger brother felt that they were as good as free.

"I want a message getting to whoever sent this, Counselor," Smith remarked when he had finished reading.

"How can I help?" Yorck demanded. "They pinned that to my host's door—"

"Likely knowing you was acting for these *hombres*," Smith interrupted. "So, you pin up a note, they'll find a way of collecting it. I'll not stop them, or bother 'em in any way."

"All right," Yorck muttered. "I'll do it."

"Maybe you'd like to write it down for me when we go back to the office?" Smith inquired. "It's this. 'Warning. If Miss Shivers and Deputy Jeffreys aren't set free and brought unharmed to the marshal's office by noon, I'll take out Virgil Jones and shoot him—!'"

"Shoot—!" Yorck croaked and Morgan Jones stopped smiling.

"'If they're still not here one hour later, I'll shoot Morgan Jones,'" Smith continued. "You write it, Counselor, and I'll sign it."

"Hey!" Morgan Jones yelped, grabbing hold of the bars.

"You can't bluff the Friends of Justice!" Yorck warned, glaring at the scared brother while addressing Smith.

"I'm not aiming to try," the Texan replied. "You don't reckon whoever's got my deputy and Miss Shivers'll let them go after I've turned this pair free, do you? They'll know too much. Who took them and where. They're dead if I obey. So I'll do what what I said."

"Nonsense!" Yorck snorted, but there was uncertainty in his voice. "You're an officer, sworn to uphold the law."

"Which I aim to do, right down the line," Smith drawled. "And giving in to threats like this's no way to do it."

"Miss Jeffreys—!" Yorck commenced, turning toward the girl.

"Don't stand arguing, you crazy son of a bitch!" Morgan screeched, trying to grab the lawyer through the bars. "Smith's not bluffing. He'll do it."

"Of course he won't—!" Yorck snapped, reversing direction and glaring at the prisoners.

Raw fear played on Morgan Jones's face. He had learned the identity of the new peace officers and knew something of their reputations. So he had no doubt that the marshal would carry out his threat.

"You get—!" Morgan yelled.

"All right. All right!" the lawyer barked. "Don't lose your head!" Waiting until Morgan had stopped speaking, he rounded on Smith. "I won't have my clients threatened in this manner!"

"There's no threat in it, Counselor," Smith replied. "Until noon they'll be treated as prisoners awaiting trial. After that it is up to the Friends of Justice."

Although he had quieted one outburst from Morgan, Yorck knew that there might be more. In his fear, the young man could easily say something that would incriminate the lawyer. Even Virgil, the older and tougher of the pair, looked nervous and uneasy.

"Marshal," Yorck said coldly. "I wish to speak in private with my clients."

"That's your privilege, Counselor," Smith replied. "We'll go and wait in my office. Just mind one thing. I won't have your host's house watched, or do anything to stop my message being collected by the *hombres* who left this letter. I don't want to kill these two fellers, but I'll do it if I have to."

"And I'll back Marshal Smith on his decision," Wil went on. "If we give in this once, it will establish a precedent that could be disastrous."

Following Smith's party from the basement, Yorck returned when he had made sure that none of them had stayed behind to listen. The cowhand, Robbie, had been released the previous night, so the lawyer and his clients were alone. Going toward the cell, Yorck could see he faced a difficult task.

"This whole damned deal's gone sour," Morgan Jones growled. "We never expected nothing like's happened."

"And we didn't expect your brother to shoot down a cowhand," Yorck replied.

"Evan only meant to throw a scare into him," Virgil protested.

"Then why didn't you get out with him?" demanded Yorck.

"We aimed to give him a head start and hold them farmers off his back," Virgil explained. "Only Smith and his deputies arrived before we could pull out."

"They come so fast and ready they must've known we was there," Morgan put in suspiciously, looking the lawyer over in a calculating manner. "You get out to the Page place and tell your pards to do like Smith says."

"I agree with Brother Morg," Virgil went on. "We wasn't told there's a bunch of gun hawks running the law. So we played along with your crowd. Only the water's over the willows now. Smith'll do what he says."

"I ain't getting shot!" Morg warned, panic in his tone. "So you get word to your pards, or I'll tell Smith where to find them and who's behind this whole deal."

"Don't be stup—!" Yorck blazed.

"Marshal!" Morgan shouted. "Hey, Marshall Smith!"

"Shut up!" the lawyer hissed. "Say anything to him and you'll ruin everything. I'll go and get the hostages fetched back. Your only hope of getting out of here is with our help."

"All right," Virgil said. "We'll give you to noon. If you've not got Lily Shivers and young Jeffreys back here by then, I'm going to start talking."

"You want something?" Smith asked, coming in.

"I will do as you say," Yorck promised. "But I warn you that I will lodge the strongest protest—"

"Time's a-wasting, Counselor," Smith warned. "If those fellers've a fair way to go, you'd best not be long in getting my message fastened to that door."

"I'll go now," the lawyer answered, throwing a long glance at the brothers. "And I hold you to your word not to jeopardize my clients by interfering with the collection of your ultimatum."

"Your clients mean nothing to me, Counselor," Smith drawled. "It's Miss Shivers and my deputy I'm interested in."

Returning to the ground floor, Yorck accepted the note which Smith had already written and left. He had only just gone when the

Texan told Ottaway to follow him. Ottaway was to keep watch, without being seen, on Yorck's activities. After the deputy had departed, Wil looked at Smith.

"You gave your word—"

"Not to stop anybody collecting that letter I gave the counselor," Smith finished for her. "I never said I wouldn't have a watch kept on him. Nobody'll come. The note he gave me hadn't been pinned to a door all night. There wasn't even a pinhole in it."

"So you think that Yorck's involved?" Wil asked.

"Up to his neck," Smith replied. "He'll go to wherever they're holding Lily and Stan, or he'll get the hell out of town. Either way, we'll have the answer."

"What if Yorck sits tight," Frith asked, "and the Joneses won't talk?"

"Then I'll do what I told them," Smith declared. "Like Miss Jeffreys told the counselor, if you once give way in this kind of a deal, you may's well kiss law and order good-bye. And I'll be damned if I'll let it happen."

Asking to be kept informed of developments, Wil left to attend to her affairs as banker. With her went the bartender, who had been asked by Smith not to talk about what he had seen and heard. Smith and Frith remained at the office, awaiting the next developments. At half past eleven, Ottaway returned.

"Yorck's just pulled out, on the eastbound stage. He's not seen anybody, nor left your letter on the door of the house where he's been staying."

"What now, Wax?" Frith inquired.

"We'll go and see the Jones boys," the Texan replied. "They've been sweating long enough. I reckon Morgan'll be ready to talk."

Hearing the clatter of boots on the stairs, the Jones brothers rose and came to the door of their cell. Although Virgil still showed little emotion, Morgan exhibited a mixture of alarm and expectancy.

"Your lawyer's caught the eastbound stage, gents," Smith remarked. "And he hasn't tried to get in touch with those fellers."

"So?" Virgil asked, nudging his brother in the ribs.

"So you're more stupid than I thought if you can't figure out what's happening," Smith replied.

"Maybe you'd best tell us," Virgil suggested.

"I think they've sold you down the river," Smith declared. "They want us to kill you."

"Why would they?" Morgan demanded, ignoring Virgil's warning glares. "They brought us here to get us our farm back."

"The hell they did," Frith snorted. "They fetched you to be used as goats, to be butchered by the ranchers so there'd be trouble through the fair. Or arrested by us. I'll bet they didn't tell you how Miss Jeffreys'd brought us in to run the law instead of the regular officers."

"They didn't," Virgil agreed, while Morgan muttered distractedly.

"How'd you reckon we got to know you was in town so quick?" Ottaway went on.

Virgil and Morgan exchanged glances. Clearly they had discussed that aspect of the affair and formed conclusions which Ottaway was apparently confirming. So Smith decided to continue rubbing home the hot iron.

"Likely they didn't expect to be so lucky as having Evan gun down the cowhand. Or maybe they did. Did the two young 'n's give you fellers any of their cigarettes?"

"They offered, but only Evan took one. I chaw and Brother Morgan rolls his own makings."

"You were the lucky ones," Frith commented. "Them cigarettes was drugged. I bet Evan acted strange after he'd smoked it."

"He did!" Virgil admitted. "You reckon them cigarettes made him act like he did, marshal?"

"They wanted one of you to make a fool play," Smith replied, "or you might've heard that Poona Woodstole didn't aim to press that slow-elking warrant as long as you kept clear of his land."

"You're the goats for sure," Ottaway drawled. "Maybe you didn't know it, but Wax Smith had somebody else pull the hostage game and he acted just like he did with you boys."

"I mind Counselor Yorck wrote to the newspapers about how no peace officer should be allowed to gun down prisoners, even if doing it did save the hostages' lives," Frith continued. "He knowed how the marshal'd act over that letter."

"Anyways," Smith said. "We figured you ought to know. 'Cause in one hour, I'll be coming to keep my word."

"It'll look like you was shot trying to escape," Frith went on. "With Yorck gone, nobody'll know different."

"Miss Jeffreys's with us on this," Smith warned. "So we can do what I said."

With that, the Texan turned as if to leave the basement. Showing an equal disregard, the deputies followed him. The alarm and concern increased on the brothers' faces. If Marshal Caster had made the threat, they would have ignored it. Waxahachie Smith and his deputies were an entirely different proposition. Hired gunfighters, they had nothing to lose and no fear of killing if doing so would achieve their ends. As Frith had pointed out, they could fake things so the brothers would appear to have died in an escape bid. So the brothers did not doubt that they would be killed at the appointed time.

"Marshal!" Virgil yelled. "What's in it for us if we tell you everything?"

"Your lives, if we get Miss Shivers and Stan Jeffreys out without them being harmed," Smith promised. "And I figure we can do that, if there's time."

"They're being held at the Page place," Virgil said. "It's about four miles north along Widow's Creek. You should be able to get up to the house without being seen, it's in thick woods and there's only them two young fellers there with Evan."

"Huh huh!" Smith grunted. "We'll go take a look. Tell me about the rest of it, Mr. Jones. Why'd you come back?"

"Yorck had us fetched to his office in Cheyenne and said he'd heard how the Grange'd refused to help us get our farm back," Virgil explained. "He allowed we should come back up here and stand our trial for slow-elking 'cause he could get us off it. Those two young fellers come to help get the farmers on our side."

"He reckoned that we'd get off with Governor Moonlight being here for the fair," Morgan went on. "Hell, we didn't want the farm for ourselves but we could sell it."

Smith could see the whole scheme now. Wanting to embarrass the Grange and stir up trouble for the ranchers, the Free Land Society had found the perfect dupes. Told the basic facts, or a distorted version of them, people might believe that the Jones family had received a raw deal. Neither the Patrons of Husbandry nor the cattlemen would have emerged in a good light from the situation created by the brothers' return. Faced with a range war, which could easily have exploded and might even yet, the governor would be compelled to take firm action. No doubt the Free Land Society, hovering like turkey vultures, hoped to gain a considerable political advantage out of the conflict.

In which case, they might have hired the men who had tried to kill Smith, Frith and Ottaway.

"Let's get going!" Smith snapped to his deputies. "The longer we wait, the more chance of the soft-shells learning things've gone wrong."

"Do you reckon we should all go, Wax?" Ottaway asked as the trio returned to the marshal's office. "This could be a trick on Yorck's part to draw us out of town and set the Joneses free."

"It could be," Smith agreed. "I reckon that Ric and me can handle it, if you'll tend to things here in town."

"You can count on me to do that," Ottaway promised.

16

Another Trail Peters Out

Daylight had come and gone several hours earlier. Seated on the floor of a small room in a log-walled house, Lily Shivers and Stanley Jeffreys watched Wymar leave the room. Neither of them knew where they had been brought, but had identified their captors as the two soft-shells and Evan Jones. Apart from checking that their bonds were secure and giving them a drink of water, the trio had ignored the blonde and Jeffreys. However, from snatches of conversation they had heard, the prisoners had gathered that they were being held as hostages.

"What do you think Wax will do, Lily?" Jeffreys inquired.

"I'm damned if I know," the blonde admitted. "Only I'll bet it will be something those three yacks don't expect."

"Damn it all!" Jeffreys groaned. "This's me done as a deputy. Wax Smith'll not want a feller who got taken by surprise twice in one day."

"I'll bet he doesn't hold it against you when he learns why. You stopped to see what was ailing a feller lying on the sidewalk and got cracked on the head from an alley. Fine lawman you'd make, walking by something like that."

"If I could only get loose!" Jeffreys growled, having told Lily how he had come to be captured when dawn's light had first showed him his fellow victim. "Damn it all, they've got me fastened with dad's old handcuffs. I've been carrying them since Wax took me on as a deputy."

"You know, Stan," Lily remarked, wanting to take the young man's thoughts from his present position. "You've surprised me.

Way you was acting since you came home from college, I never expected to see you take on as a deputy."

"Didn't reckon Wil Jeffreys's kid brother could amount to anything without big sister's help, huh?"

"I always figured you could, if you made a stab at it. And don't forget, I've near on been Wil Jeffreys's little sister for a lot of years," Lily replied, then grinned. "Way things turned out when we tangled, I'm still that way."

"You sure tied into each other," Jeffreys smiled. "I wouldn't've expected it of Wil."

"Do you reckon I'd've got into a fight with her if I had?"

"I reckon you might. Lily. I'm sorry about the way I acted the night Wax hit town. Except that it made me think, that and the way he acted next day at Wil's office. I started to see myself as other folks saw me and I didn't like it. Trouble is that I've no head for the banking business and, anyway, nobody took me seriously with Wil around. So I decided to make a stab at being a lawman. Dad was pretty good at that, so I've always been told."

"He was real good," Lily agreed. "Only I bet he made mistakes when he was first starting, just like you."

At that moment the blonde realized that Jeffreys was not listening to her. Instead, he had turned his gaze to the room's window which had long since lost its glass and drapes.

"There's a horse coming," Jeffreys said. "Just one and being ridden without trying to hide it."

Wriggling onto his back, he rolled toward the window. There, he writhed around until he was sitting supported by the wall. By bracing his back against the logs and forcing on the floor with his feet, he eased himself erect. Still leaning against the wall, he peered cautiously out of the window. He did not find an enlightening view awaiting his efforts. Fairly thick woods flanked the side of the house and, he assumed, surrounded it. There was, however, a small and winding path approaching the building within his range of vision and a rider was coming along it.

While Jeffreys had been completing his observations, Lily had joined him. Although every movement had been agony and she presented a disheveled appearance due to rolling on a dirty floor, she pressed her right shoulder against the wall and let out a low hiss as she identified the newcomer.

"It's that soft-shell law-wrangler, Yorck," Lily growled. "He's the bastard who set me up for this. I was going home and he called to me. Like a fool, I stood with my back to the alley by the end of the Bull. Next thing I knew, a flour sack was over my head and I couldn't do a blasted thing."

"He looks like something's put a burr in his britches," Jeffreys commented.

"Or somebody," the blonde corrected.

"Did you get them?" Wymar asked, appearing from beyond the end of the building and striding to meet the lawyer.

"No," Yorck replied. "Smith refused to give them to me."

"You weren't followed here?" the younger man demanded.

"Do you think I'm a fool?" the lawyer snorted and dismounted. "Hold your voice down, damn it."

"What's wrong?" Wymar said, in a softer tone.

"Smith says he'll kill the Jones brothers if we don't turn Jeffreys and the saloon woman loose."

Although the speakers had moderated their tones, the words carried to Lily's and Jeffreys's ears. They looked at each other briefly and in a startled manner. Neither of them had expected Smith to yield to the soft-shells' demands, but would never have expected him to take such a line of refusal.

Dropping their voices to a level which did not carry to the listeners, Yorck and Wymar adopted a conspiratorial air as they continued the conversation. Throwing glances at the front of the cabin, but not to where their prisoners watched them, they argued briefly. Studying the pair, Jeffreys decided that Yorck's proposals did not meet with Wymar's approval. Then the young soft-shell seemed to give way and accept. Pointing to the building, Wymar returned the way he had come and the lawyer followed leading his horse.

"You've got to hand it to Wax Smith," Lily said quietly. "He says and does the damndest things."

"Sure," Jeffreys agreed. "Only we'd best get sat down and not let them know we've been listening. They'll be coming for us soon, unless I miss my guess."

Turning their backs to the wall, Lily and Jeffreys shuffled down into a sitting position. They had hardly done so before the door opened and the two soft-shells entered. Taking a jackknife from his pocket, Landers cut the bonds holding the prisoners' ankles.

"Get up," Wymar ordered.

"You'll have to help me," Lily replied.

"Do it," Wymar told his companion, pulling a Smith & Wesson New Model 32 revolver from his jacket pocket. "If they try anything, I'll kill them."

Putting away his knife, Landers helped the blonde to rise. When his turn came to be assisted, Jeffreys fought down his inclination to use his knee in the appropriate place on his helper. While he felt sure he could incapacitate Landers, Wymar held a revolver. Only a .32 caliber, maybe, but lethal enough at close range. And even if he succeeded in subduing the two young soft-shells, the sound of the disturbance would bring Yorck and Evan Jones to investigate.

No. The time for resistance had not yet come. So Jeffreys allowed himself to be shoved through the door after Lily.

They entered what had been the main living room of the cabin. Now its only furnishings were three open bedrolls—on the center of them lay Evan Jones's Ballard rifle—at the left of the room and two more on the right. Jones stood with Yorck in the center of the room and looked at the prisoners in a calculating manner.

"Your friend, the marshal, isn't such a good friend after all," the lawyer announced, standing with his right hand hidden beneath the left side of his jacket. "He won't trade your lives for Mr. Jones's brothers."

"So I'm going to help him change his mind," Evan Jones went on.

"You mean the counselor hasn't told you the truth?" Jeffreys inquired.

"What'd that be?" Jones asked.

"Waxahachie Smith's going to shoot your brothers if we're not set free," Jeffreys explained. "Look at Yorck's face if you think I'm lying."

Jones swung his gaze in the lawyer's direction, seeing shock and anger that he interpreted as an admission that Jeffreys had told the truth. Realizing that he had confirmed the young farmer's suspicions, Yorck tried to turn aside the storm of protests which he knew would be forthcoming.

"Smith's bluffing!" the lawyer said, backing toward the door.

"Believe me, Evan," Jeffreys injected. "Wax Smith doesn't bluff unless he's ready to back his play if he gets called. Unless we're set free, your brothers—"

"Shut up!" Wymar screeched, leaping in front of the speaker and brandishing his revolver. "I'll kill you if you say another word."

Watching the soft-shell, Lily knew that he meant what he said. Deprived of the marijuana on which he had come to depend, Wymar was in a state of hysterical rage that might easily burst. For all that, the blonde did not hesitate to draw his attention from Wil's brother.

"And that'll get Virgil and Morgan killed for sure, Evan," Lily warned. "Don't forget that they were captured so you could escape."

"Quiet!" Wymar howled, swinging the revolver from Jeffreys to Lily. "I'm going to—"

Whatever path young Jeffreys might have been following since his return to Widow's Creek, he showed that he could play the man when the need arose. Stepping swiftly behind Wymar, he pivoted and lashed his right leg around. In college, he had taken an interest in various forms of self-defense and put his training to good use. The toe of his boot took the soft-shell in the kidney region with considerable force. With a croaking yell of agony, Wymar arched his back. Instead of carrying out his threat against Lily, he dropped his Smith & Wesson, stumbled by her and fell sobbing near the wall.

Landers let out a squawk of alarm and bent to grab for the revolver. Jumping at him, Jones crashed a fist against the back of his neck. Down went Landers, collapsing like a rabbit with its spinal column broken, to land on top of the weapon. Seeing that he could not gain possession of the Smith & Wesson, Jones turned to run to where his Ballard rifle lay on his bedroll.

"Look out!" Lily yelled, springing so that she placed herself between Jeffreys and the lawyer.

Giving their attention to the soft-shells, Jeffreys and Jones had failed to keep Yorck under observation. The lawyer brought his right hand into view, holding a short-barreled Merwin & Hulbert Army Pocket revolver. Even as Lily gave her warning, he cocked, lined and fired it.

Not at Jeffreys, but making Jones his target. Struck between the shoulders with the .45 bullet, the young farmer blundered into the wall and slid downward.

"Get back!" Yorck snarled as Jeffreys lunged by Lily. Reaching behind him, the lawyer drew open the door and backed through it. "This couldn't have worked out better for me."

"How come?" Jeffreys asked, playing for time as he skidded to a halt.

"When they find you bunch dead, there'll be no stopping the war that'll blow up between the ranchers and farmers," Yorck explained.

"Those two as well as Jones, Lily and me?"

"All of you. If the Grange try to keep the peace, their own people will turn against them and to us."

"That's not why you'll kill us," Jeffreys challenged. "You're doing it so there'll be no witnesses."

"That's true," the lawyer confessed. "I'll go back with the tragic news that you'd been killed by Wymar, Jones and Landers in their drugged rage. Then Smith will shoot the other two and the Free Land Society will have its martyrs. By the time we're through, the Grange will be a thing of the—"

Chopping off his words, Yorck tried to follow Jeffreys with the short barrel of his revolver. Waiting until the lawyer had got into his full flow of rhetoric, the young man flung himself away from Lily. Jeffreys heard the Merwin & Hulbert crack and the sound of its bullet whizzing by his head. Then he tried to reach the lawyer before the other could recock the revolver. Showing surprising speed, Yorck leapt back and slammed the door.

"It's no good, Jeffreys!" he yelled. "I can get you from the windows."

The sound of running footsteps caused Yorck to swing around. Carrying his *kukri*, Poona Woodstole came from the trees and,

with Zorin Bilak at his side, made for the lawyer. Spluttering out
curses, Yorck tried to swing around his revolver. Whipping back
his right hand, Woodstole threw the *kukri* on the move. Hissing
through the air, its heavy blade passed between Yorck's ribs and
sank into the vital organs beyond them.

Halfway to the door, Jeffreys saw it opening slowly. Yorck staggered back into the room. Falling face up, he lay with the fancy
black hilt of the *kukri* rising from his chest. Having drawn his
revolver, Woodstole hurdled the body. Also gripping a Colt, Bilak
followed the Englishman. They arrived ready for trouble, but met
none. Sprawled on his bedroll, Jones was dead. Landers groaned
his way back to consciousness. Whimpering in fright and pain,
Wymar crouched on the floor and stared around him.

"Are you all right, Lily?" Woodstole inquired, holstering his
Colt.

"Sure," answered the pallid-faced girl.

"How about you, Stan?" the Englishman went on.

"He didn't hit me," Jeffreys replied. "But I'm near on scared to
death."

"Don't you believe *that*," Lily protested. "Wax Smith
couldn't've handled things any better. Say. How'd you boys come
to be here just when we needed you?"

"We got together, without telling anybody, as soon as we heard
what had happened," Woodstole explained. "Gave some thought
to where they might have taken you and came to take a look."

"Where's Charlie?" the blonde inquired.

"He's with Mr. Cushman—" Woodstole began.

"That high-up Grange feller?" Lily gasped.

"Yes," Bilak grinned, having leathered his revolver and stepped
behind her to free her hands. "It turns out that they both served in
Hood's Brigade during the War and they're getting on like a house
on fire. They're checking on another deserted farm right now."

Searching the unprotesting soft-shells, Woodstole found the key
for the handcuffs and released Jeffreys. The young man made use
of them to secure Wymar to Landers. Waiting until Woodstole had
retrieved the *kukri*, Jeffreys escorted the soft-shells from the build-

ing and made them sit with their backs to the wall. Lily and Bilak had already come out.

"Hey, fellers," the blonde said. "These unsociable bastards didn't know how to treat a lady. I'm hungry. Shall we see if they've anything to eat, or head for town and get a decent meal?"

"I'm for going back to town," Woodstole stated.

"From what we heard Yorck telling this feller," Jeffreys went on, indicating Wymar, "I'd say we should get back as fast as we can. If we don't, the Joneses are going to wish we had."

"Look after this pair, Stan," Bilak suggested. "We'll pick up our horses."

"If you need a gun—," Woodstole offered.

"Unless they left it in town, my own's here some place," Jeffreys answered, and glared at the soft-shells. "Where is it?"

"In my bedroll," Landers yelped. "This wasn't my idea—"

"I hope the judge agrees with you," Jeffreys sniffed, and entered the cabin to return strapping on his gun belt. He checked the revolver's loads and continued, "I reckon I can handle things now."

Going to where they had left their mounts before stalking up to the cabin, Woodstole and Bilak led them back. Then the two men helped saddle the horses used by Jones and the two soft-shells. Leaving the bodies inside the building, the party mounted. Jeffreys had released Wymar and Landers, but they gave no trouble and showed no sign of trying to escape. In fact, from what they had said to Jeffreys, they were willing to tell the whole story behind their actions if doing so would help reduce their sentences when they stood trial.

Before the party had covered half the distance to town, they saw Smith and Frith riding toward them at a fast trot. Jeffreys felt worried as he watched the pair approaching, wondering how they would take the news that he had once again fallen into a trap.

Greetings were exchanged and the marshal asked for explanations of the other party's presence. Giving Jeffreys no time to reply, Lily launched into the story of her kidnapping and finished with a description of his behavior in the main room of the cabin. The account was very creditable to Jeffreys, but he was uneasy when

Smith turned an impersonal gaze his way. Sucking in breath, Jeffreys told how he had been caught and watched for signs of condemnation on the two men's faces.

"I reckon you'd best team up with me for a spell, Stan," Frith remarked.

"It'd be best," Smith agreed. "You've got things to learn, *amigo,* and Ottaway's not the man to teach you."

To Jeffreys, it seemed that a great weight had been lifted from him. Instead of condemning him and discarding him as useless, Smith and Frith would still allow him to stay on as a deputy. More than that, they were willing to give him instruction in his duties. Pleasant company though he had been, Ottaway had never offered to do so.

"So you're the bunch who've been trying to get Wax and me killed," Frith growled, moving his horse toward the soft-shells.

"W—We didn't mean Miss Shivers and Mr. Jeffreys any harm!" Wymar whined. "It was Yorck's idea to kidnap them as hostages and he said we should kill them."

"Oh sure!" Frith snorted. "And it was Yorck hired the fellers who came hunting Wax and me?"

"I don't know what you mean!" Wymar whimpered.

"Since Miss Jeffreys hired us, we've both had men come to where we was and try to gun us down," Frith elaborated. "That ought to make it clear enough, even for college boys like you."

"I wasn't involved in that!" Wymar insisted. "Honest I wasn't!"

"How about you?" Smith demanded, glaring at the second soft-shell.

"Me!" Landers yelped. "I—We—I didn't even know that Miss Jeffreys had hired kil—you—you gentlemen until we got here. We were told that there'd only be the usual kind of local peace officers to deal with."

"That's right, marshal!" Wymar went on. "If we'd known about you being here, we wouldn't've tried this trick."

"Reckon they're telling the truth, Wax?" Frith inquired.

"They're too scared to be lying," Smith decided, after looking at the pair for a few seconds. "Of course, they might not've known what Yorck was doing. He could've done the hiring."

"Except that he didn't know we'd been taken on," Frith countered. " 'Least, he acted like he didn't when he first came to the office. Say, though. How did he get out to the farm?"

"On the bay Lily's riding," Jeffreys supplied.

"He could've left the stage a couple of miles out of town, sneaked back and got it," Frith said quietly, turning his gaze to the bay. "Only it's not been ridden hard today."

"Which it'd've had to have been to get him here in the time," Smith went on, also taking in the horse's appearance. "And if he didn't take the stage—Stan, what sort of things did Ottaway ask you?"

"How do you mean?" Jeffreys inquired.

"What'd you talk about?" Smith elaborated. "Did he ever want to know anything about the bank?"

"He only asked if Wil was thinking of taking any special precautions to guard it when the money for the fair started piling up. I used to tell him he'd have to ask Wil about that."

"Did he know either Ric or me was coming?"

"Sure, Wax. Wil told him as soon as she heard. He kept asking, so that he could get some more men if you couldn't come."

"He never asked you about the jewelry Poona's cousin was bringing?"

"No, Ric," Jeffreys replied. "Hey, though! He used to hint that there might be some attractions that Wil hadn't let on about. I knew that she wanted Sir Basil's jewels kept a secret and thought she was having Tal try me out to see if I could keep it that way. So I used to say I didn't know anything. You don't think—?"

"When one trail peters out, you have to look for another," Smith replied. "Ottaway knew we were coming and where to find us. With us out of the way, he could hire his own men. The bank'll be busting at the seams with money comes the end of the fair. Only we've whittled his hired help down some. Does he have any friends around town, Stan? Fellers he sees regular, I mean."

"Only the undertaker," Jeffreys replied.

"Who?" Smith snapped.

"A small, miserable-looking feller," Jeffreys explained. "He's not been around town for more than two or three days. I don't know if he is an undertaker, but he looks like one. I've seen Tal talking to him a couple of times after he's sent me off to handle chores on my own."

17

The Tall Man and
the Short Man's Plan

With a sense of quiet satisfaction, Talbot Ottaway rode toward the center bridge. He sat on a big, powerful horse and led a second, equally as well-made and capable of long, fast traveling. So far, no alarm had been raised from the bank. That did not entirely surprise him. Wil Jeffreys and the Pinkerton guard were in no position to announce that the bank had been robbed.

In a way, though, it was a pity that Ottaway could not have treated Otis M. Capey better. After all, the little man had been the one behind the plan. The trouble was that Capey could not ride well enough for the fast flight which must be made if Ottaway hoped to avoid capture.

It had all begun some time back, while Ottaway was taking pay in a railroad right-of-way war. Capey had arrived with a proposition. A successful Eastern criminal, he had been employed as a servant at the British Embassy in Washington, where he had been planning to steal a valuable collection of jewelry. He had been unable to make any progress until he had discovered that their owner had been asked to put them on display at a county fair to be held in Widow's Creek.

Guessing that his opportunity would be greater in Wyoming, Capey had headed west. By some means or other, he had been put into contact with Ottaway. Between them, they had hatched a plot not only to gain possession of the jewels but to rob the bank of the money deposited during the fair.

Quitting his job, Ottaway had gone to Widow's Creek. There he had made the acquaintance of the lady mayor and persuaded Wil Jeffreys to hire a special police force. That was when things had started to go wrong. Ottaway had suggested men he knew would not be available, in the hope that he could bring in the gang he and Capey had gathered to act as deputies. With them running the law, the rest of the plan would have been easy. Wil had sent for two men, efficient peace officers and smart enough to smell a rat. So the conspirators had decided to stop Smith and Frith reaching the town.

Using the information Ottaway had gathered from Wil, two parties had left to intercept Smith and Frith. Neither had met with any success. Capey had been at the stagecoach way station when the try at Smith had failed. Wanting to make sure that Hardy's party carried nothing to hint at what was planned, he had pretended to be an undertaker and helped search the bodies. Left alone at the barn, he had cut the girths on Smith's saddle to prevent the Texan arriving unexpectedly in Widow's Creek. Knowing that Smith would be curious about the attempt on his life, Capey had written a message on a page from his notebook and, by placing it under another sheet, imprinted a name on it. He had selected Poona Woodstole as the only person, other than Ottaway, he knew in the town.

One of Ottaway's tasks had been to learn when the jewelry was to arrive. Although he had cultivated Stanley Jeffreys, he had gained nothing from that source. Jeffreys either could not, or would not, discuss his sister's affairs.

Capey had acted on his own initiative when sending the Sheppey brothers after Smith. Then, deciding that the Texan would be suspicious if he discovered that nobody had tried to kill Ottaway, he had told Dilkes to fire a shot at the deputy. Thinking that Ottaway knew of this, Dilkes had obeyed and had been killed. When Ottaway had gone to see Capey, bristling with suspicion, the small man had pointed out that they could no longer hope to rob the bank at the end of the fair, so the man was better out of the way. Ottaway had been inclined to believe the explanation. If Capey had hoped to achieve anything, he needed Ottaway's help. The deputy's actions when the soft-shells had tried to break up the meeting gained Smith's grudging confidence. So Ottaway could be present at meetings, picking up information and—as he had done when Hardy's visit to Wil's office had been mentioned—ready to change the subject if the possibility of a bank holdup should be approached.

On hearing that the Big Indian and Jed Trotter were coming on Monday, Ottaway had known that the attempt must be made before then. He had deliberately allowed Evan Jones to escape in the hope of stirring up trouble between the ranchers and farmers. This had not materialized, but the kidnappings had been the break he needed. Instead of reporting to Smith as soon as he had seen Yorck riding out of town, he had visited Capey and arranged that they should make their move. Taking his false information to the marshal's office, he had fixed it for himself to be left behind when Smith had set off on the rescue bid. That had not been difficult, for he had guessed that the marshal would take Frith rather than him when headed into danger.

After that, everything had been simple. Collecting the horses Ottaway had selected for their escape, the two conspirators had gone to the bank. A look through the front window had told them that Ryall was making one of his visits to a girl in a whorehouse across the river and the junior teller was working at his desk. So they had gone to the side door, where Ottaway gained admittance under the pretense of having brought Capey to be hired as a special deputy.

There had been one Pink-Eye present and a fast-drawn Colt crashing onto his head put him out of the deal. Acting no less quickly, Capey had laid an open razor against Wil's throat and ordered her to be silent. A smart young woman, she had seen the futility of resistance and obeyed. Then, under the threat of having the guard and her teller murdered with the razor, she had been forced to open the safe. With Wil and the guard securely bound and gagged—to prevent any warning reaching the unsuspecting teller in the front room—Capey had fetched in the saddlebags left outside the side door to avoid arousing suspicion. A blow from the barrel of Ottaway's Colt had tumbled the small man unconscious.

For a few seconds, Ottaway had debated whether to kill all three of his victims. Moral scruples did not come into his decision of sparing their lives. Public opinion would be more severe against a man who murdered a "good" woman in cold blood than at a mere bank robber. Nor would the Pinkerton Agency ever cease in their efforts to hunt down the murderer of one of their men. That left Capey. He knew the escape plan, which was why he did not die. When he told Smith that Ottaway intended to make for the Canadian border, the hunt would be concentrated in that direction. So Ottaway would head south, riding relay and traveling faster than any posse, each man of which had only one horse. He knew enough about the crooked trails to be safe, and the money from the bank's safe, while much less than would have been in it by the end of the fair, would set him up comfortably somewhere safe.

Riding high on a cloud of happy thoughts, with his horses' hooves drumming on the planks of the center bridge, Ottaway was suddenly brought down to earth with a bump.

Waxahachie Smith rode his lathered *bayo-lobo* from an alley on the street ahead of Ottaway. There was no hope of turning back and avoiding the Texan, so Ottaway raised his left hand in a greeting.

"What's up, Wax?"

"They weren't at the Page place," Smith replied, riding forward as Ottaway halted his mounts on the bridge.

"Yeah. I know," the man agreed. "I thought they might be lying, so I sneaked downstairs on tippy-toe and listened at the basement door. Morgan let on that you'd never think of looking at the Renner farm."

"So you got a spare horse and came looking for me?"

"Sure. These were the only two decent mounts at the barn. Where's Ric?"

"That blasted critter they gave him threw a shoe," Smith drawled. "Afore we go, maybe we'd best let Miss Jeffreys know what's happened."

"Is there time?" Ottaway inquired.

"We'll just have to make time," Smith declared. "Turn around and let's go."

"You're the marshal," Ottaway replied. "Hey! Your hoss looks hard-rid. Why don't you take this one now?"

"I might as well," Smith admitted, gripping the saddle horn

with his gloved left hand as he swung over his right leg to dismount.

Instantly Ottaway commenced his draw. With his fingers closing about the butt of his revolver, he started to form an uneasy impression that something was badly wrong. Instead of merely getting down, Smith had thrown himself clear of the *bayo-lobo*. While he was still in the air, the Texan's right hand made a white flash as it snapped toward the staghorn grips of the Colt slip gun.

A *white* flash!

Yet Smith's left hand was covered by the brown leather of its glove.

That meant the right hand must be bare!

Smith only removed his gloves, exposing his mutilated hands, when expecting trouble and he might need to use his gun. So he either suspected or knew that Ottaway had been playing a treacherous game.

Out flashed Ottaway's revolver; but the shock of his discovery caused him to hesitate before he turned loose a shot. As soon as he depressed the trigger and released the hammer, he sensed that he had missed. So he began to draw back the hammer and turn the barrel into line on the Texan.

Hearing the scream of Ottaway's bullet passing close above his head, Smith landed on his feet and holding his weapon. No other kind of single-action revolver could equal a slip gun for speed of fire. Three times in one and a half seconds, his thumb operated the stubby hammer spur. Coming on the heels of Ottaway's attempt, the trio of detonations merged into what appeared to be a continuous sound. All nine balls raked into the man's chest, almost ripping him in half. Startled by the noise and muzzle blasts, the two horses belonging to Ottaway reared on their hind legs. Thrown from the saddle, he fell onto the bridge's guardrail and from it into the water.

Allowing his own horse to lope away, Smith barred the progress of Ottaway's relay. He sprang forward and his left hand caught the reins of the animal the man had been riding. Ignoring the shouts which rose and the sight of people running toward him, Smith concentrated on bringing the frightened horses under control. Jeffreys and Frith galloped their horses along the bank of the river, converging on the marshal. By the time they arrived, he was standing alongside the calmed animals and was looking into one of the saddlebags.

"Did you call it right, Wax?" Jeffreys asked.

On hearing of Ottaway's connection with Capey, Smith had guessed that there was a plot to steal the Houghton-Rand jewels. So he had asked Woodstole and Bilak to escort Lily and the prisoners into town while he and his deputies pushed on as fast as they could. On reaching the outskirts, Smith had sent Frith upstream and Jeffreys down to cover all three bridges between them. Seeing Ottaway approaching, without the other being aware of his own presence, Smith had hidden in the alley and made his appearance when the man was on the bridge.

"I called it right," Smith confirmed, closing the bag. "Ric. Head for the bank fast. Stan, fetch Ottaway out of the water."

"That's the best of being the youngest deputy, Stan," Frith commented. "You get all the easy chores."

Although Jeffreys was worried about his sister's welfare, he obeyed Smith's order. Not until the body had been delivered to the undertaker's shop did the young man have the opportunity to go and find out what had happened to her.

Any doubts about the identity of the men behind the attempts to kill Smith and Frith were ended when Capey regained consciousness at the jail. Led by Smith to believe that Ottaway was still alive, the small man told the full story so that his treacherous accomplice would also be implicated.

"Well," said Jeffreys, as he, Smith and Frith sat in the marshal's office after attending to the incarceration of Capey and the two soft-shells, "we've got everything settled and quieted down now."

"Sure," Smith agreed. "And it's up to us to see that it stays that way."

"There's only one thing I'd like to know," Frith remarked. "How come every time you make up one of your fancy laws you use the same set of numbers?"

"You mean eleven, twenty-three, and sixty-one?" Smith asked.

"Them's the ones," agreed Frith. "What are they?"

"The date of the day I was born," Smith explained.